The Scarlet Oak

Cover design by Elle Staples

Cover illustration by Lydia Colburn

First published in 1938

This unabridged version has updated grammar and spelling.

Table of Contents

CHAPTER 1

Wind Across New Jersey

The two boys had got up very early, awakened, perhaps, by the high spring wind which was shaking the windows and banging the shutters one after another all the length of the house. They had seen so little of the place when they arrived the night before in the dark that it had all the excitement of exploring to come down the broad staircase, pull back the bolts of the front door, and come on the wide terrace. They stood still and Hugh said, "Oh!" And after a moment he added, "This is what America looks like, then. I hadn't remembered."

It was late last night that they and their mother had come to Grandfather's house, outside Bordentown in the state of New Jersey. It was pouring rain when they came in out of the dark, to be greeted by Grandfather smiling in the doorway, and Nannie, his housekeeper, standing beside him and ducking a curtsy so quickly and suddenly that one could hardly see her do it. Their mother had told them that was just what she would do. High-shouldered old Jackson, who was Grandfather's man and married to Nannie, and who had once been a sailor, picked up their bags and kept saying over and over, "Bless you now, Miss Eleanor. Bless

you that you've come with your boys back to this house."
Even though Grandfather said so little, everything made
them all feel so fully and warmly welcomed. It was hard to
believe that only yesterday morning their ship had been
tacking back and forth in the Delaware River, to land them
at the port of Philadelphia.

And in the days before that, weeks of them, they had
been voyaging across from France, a short, easy voyage,
the Captain had said, only thirty-five days out of Bordeaux,
in this year of 1817, now that the long wars were over. The
journey from Philadelphia in the jolting coach had showed
nothing but rain streaming down the coach windows, so
that, after all, this view from the terrace was the first sight
of America, or at least of such part of it as went by the
name of New Jersey.

It was good country, Hugh thought, wide country falling
away in a gentle slope to the broad plain, spreading far,
rolling a little, dropping into tree-marked fallows where
streams were twisting, dotted with groves of trees and with
farmhouses, the smoke of whose chimneys was all going
up in the early morning, and all blowing the same way
before the high March wind.

Jeremy did not stand so long to look, for he could
recollect something of all this from their last visit. He
walked down, past the row of windows that belonged to
the library inside, and came to the end of the terrace. "I
thought I remembered," he said. "That is the workshop
there under the chestnut tree, the place where we were
making the kite."

They crossed the grass and tried the latch of the door,

which opened under Jeremy's hand. It was a little building with a long bench, with the level sun streaming in at the east window, with the rows of tools hung neatly in their places, and with, strange to relate, the kite lying there in its place just as Jeremy had left it, eight years before. The boys could hardly believe it, but there it was, laid out carefully and weighted down, so that it would not warp. Its frame of balsa wood was a little discolored by time, but neatly bent and tied and fitted for the making of the largest kite that, so far, had ever been designed to fly above the windy meadows of New Jersey. "The wood ought to be well seasoned by now," Jeremy said.

The eight years since their visit to this place had brought many things. Jeremy Armond was seventeen now, and Hugh was twelve. Hugh could not remember having been there at all, and Jeremy could not recall a great deal, so much had come between. He did remember how he and Grandfather planned the kite, how Grandfather had sent word to one of his ship's captains to bring home balsa wood from South America, very light and strong, to make the frame. But the kite was never finished. Work on it was interrupted that day when there arrived a letter from the boys' father, who, although he was an American, lived in France because of his business. The letter said that the Emperor Napoleon, who sat on the French throne, was planning another war, and immediately their mother packed up hastily to catch the ship that lay in the Delaware and go back to him. If there was to be a war she did not want the sea to lie between them.

And then so many things happened, one after another.

The wars had ended at last, with the great battle of
Waterloo and the downfall of Napoleon from his high
place. He had made so many wars, and they were all to
be for the glory of France, so he declared. In the same
month as the battle of Waterloo, the boys' father died in
Paris. Their mother stayed in France for two years more,
because of Jeremy's school at Neuilly which she wanted
him to finish. They used to talk about America and how
everything must be so peaceful and quiet there, after once
America's own war with England came to an end. But
those times seemed not to have been so peaceful for Mr.
Hiram Nicolls, the boys' grandfather, for he had spent
most of his time in Philadelphia, close to his shipping
offices, and very little in the country where he was most
truly happy. He had plainly had no time at all for his
workshop, so there the kite still lay. Grandfather must have
given orders that it was not to be moved but was to be kept
there for the boys when they should come back.

When anyone comes to stay in a new place, there is
usually a little while, a very little while, when he does
not know quite what to do with himself. If the boys had
wondered, it was clear to them now just what they could
do first.

"We could finish the kite in half an hour, if Nannie can
give us paper and paste and string," Jeremy said. "This is
just the kind of day to fly it."

The kitchen door was under a little vine-covered porch,
at the rear of the house. As they came round the corner
of the wing, they could see the broad river, just beginning
to gleam like steel in the rising light of morning, for the

back of the house looked out toward the Delaware. Hugh happened to be first at the door, wondered if he ought to knock, and heard someone stirring inside as he waited a moment. Then he opened the door, but, after one startled look, staggered back against his brother. He was not frightened, no, but he was simply too astonished to be frightened by the strange thing that they both saw inside.

For in that deep shadowy room, with no light except the uncertain flicker of the newly kindled fire, Jackson was standing in the middle of the floor with a great pistol in his hand, a long and heavy weapon pointed straight at the door. The fact that his hand was shaking violently made the pistol seem more dangerous than if it were held with steady aim. "You can't come in. No person can come into the house this day," he roared, in a voice that the boys would never have thought was in him.

The two were so thunderstruck that they could not say a word, but stood staring. Suddenly Jackson's wrinkled old face went blank with surprise. Then, as he lowered the pistol, Nannie peered over his shoulder and cried out, "Now who would have thought that it would be the two young gentlemen coming in? And we with our minds so set that it was going to be someone else."

"But what is it? What did you expect?" Jeremy asked, still astonished.

The old woman came close to him. "There's bad news coming to the house, coming this very day," she said, nodding her head, and speaking hardly above a whisper. "But the one that brings it shall not get speech with your grandfather, not if there's anything we can do to stop him."

"But what bad news?" Hugh insisted. "How do you know what he doesn't know?"

"Oh, people like us know things by one person telling another, like," Nannie explained, though not very clearly. "People like you and your grandfather get tidings by the post rider or a messenger coming. If we could only keep it from him!"

Hugh's face was clouded and puzzled. "Is it bad that we came, Nannie?" he asked. "So many times he wrote Mother and wanted us to come here to live with him. And now we've come, was it wrong? Can't we help him?"

"It's good indeed that you came and your dear mother, but it's no help you can give, I fear," Nannie answered. "No, don't ask me more questions, for I will not tell you."

Since, then, there was nothing to be learned, the boys explained what they had come for. Nannie gave directions to Jackson:

"There's paper that I saved from around the sugar loaves, good blue thin paper that would be just the thing. And you'll find a ball of heavy cord in the cupboard, but it was for the garden and the dear Lord knows where we'd get another if they don't give it safe back to me. Now one minute more while I stir you up a bowl of flour paste."

Jackson had said not a word, but he put away the pistol on the cupboard shelf and brought out the ball of cord. The two boys went back to the shop with their arms full.

It was less than an hour later that they came out on the terrace, with the big blue kite held carefully between them. The wind snatched at it, so that it was hard to hold it safe from being broken. Hugh straightened out the long tail. "Now," said Jeremy, and tossed it into the air while Hugh ran down the terrace with the string. The kite hesitated an instant, trembled, then began to tower and soar, and was off upward, climbing high and tugging hard at the cord. Once it wavered, shuddered slightly, and threatened to turn head downward and dash itself to destruction on the ground as kites love to do, but another draft of air took it and it went up again.

They were so absorbed in watching, with both of their faces turned upward, that they hardly noticed when the long window near them opened and their mother came out. Eleanor Armond was tall, like her sons, with reddish golden hair that shone in the uncertain sunlight. The boys glanced round at her; they both knew that grave look that was seen upon her face only when she was anxious.

"I am troubled about your grandfather," she said to them at once. "He does not seem to be ill, but certainly he is changed from what he has always been before. And—the house and garden—nothing is like what it used to be."

The boys looked at each other. They had exchanged no talk about this place of Grandfather's, simply because there was so much to say. Whatever they remembered or did not remember, certainly they could not help noticing last night that the inside of the house, though spotlessly clean, was so bare as to be almost desolate. The long building of whitewashed brick on its ridge above the Delaware was stately still, but strangely shabby; and the garden with its white stone walls was untended, full of unkempt grass and stalks of last year's weeds. Instead of four or five men and women working in the house or at the stables, there were only Nannie and Jackson, thin, hard-working—and afraid of something. But while the three stood, with an unspoken question between them, there was a step inside and Grandfather's voice called, clear and very cheerful. "Good morning. They seem to teach you to rise early in France."

He was a handsome man, with black eyebrows and snow-white hair, and a thin, commanding face. But he looked—tired, perhaps—certainly anxious. His daughter went straight up to him.

"Father, there is something that has gone wrong. You must tell us."

He shook his head, but the smile vanished. "Nothing, there is nothing. I have been rather hard worked through these last years, that is all. What could be wrong when I have you with me at last, you and the boys, after I have asked for so long that you should come?"

Very abruptly he turned and went in; he had not even commented on the wonderful kite. The boys' mother followed him. She looked back over her shoulder at Jeremy; she wanted him to come also. To Hugh she said, "It would be a shame to pull it down when it is sailing so grandly. We'll call you in to breakfast presently." She and Jeremy disappeared into the house.

Hugh let out more and more cord; he wanted to be able to tell Jeremy that the kite had flown to the very farthest height that the string would allow. The ball was all unwound, and the very weight of the long cord was holding the kite steady, so that it no longer tugged at his hand. The wind was coming up, stronger but less even; the kite bowed and balanced as the gusts took it. And then, suddenly, a stronger puff had swept it upward and Hugh, intent on watching it climb, had let the cord slip out of his hand. It trailed away across the brown grass, down the slope. It did not move very fast; he could surely catch it.

No one who has not chased a kite moving in a full wind of late March has any idea of what a cross-country run it can be. Hugh would almost catch the trailing string, but always with a little jerk and a jump it would be just out of his reach. It got to the far edge of the garden; it had trailed over the wall into the meadow beyond. Hugh, dashing after it, always looking up, had run across the meadow and plunged headforemost through the hedge on the other side. He had no notion of what was beyond the thick bushes, but it was at a cry of surprise from two voices that he jumped back from almost under the feet of a pair of stout horses, while the coachman who was driving the chaise drew them to their haunches. The window of the vehicle flew open and a stout gentleman with a high-crowned gray hat put out his head.

"What—is anything wrong? Oh, a kite! Jump on the step, boy. John, whip up the horses. We'll get it; it's going straight down the lane."

They had almost overtaken it when a new gust of wind swung it aside into a field. Hugh dropped off the step so abruptly that he rolled into the ditch, but picked himself up and, remembering very suddenly indeed that there was such a thing as manners, jerked his best bow and said, "Merci." He had not meant to offer his thanks in French, but habit was too strong for him. The gentleman leaned out of the window, grinning.

"You're from France, eh? Then you'd better go down the road and call on Mr. Bonaparte." The chaise had carried him past.

Hugh dashed across the field; the kite was moving far ahead of him now. It was getting into stronger wind; the string was lifting above the ground. He darted at it frantically, saw a wall seem to rise up before him, a low wall at the top of a slope. He scrambled onto it, saw to his surprise that it was very high on the other side, could not stop himself, and went sprawling upon a newly dug flower bed. The kite mounted upward, flipped the string over the top of a shed and disappeared. A voice beside him said, speaking rather slowly:

"I hope you didn't hurt yourself. I am sure you can get the kite back some way."

He was in a garden, but, unlike Grandfather's, it was coming into bloom, with early daffodils along the walls, and narcissus in the cold frames sending out clouds of sweetness. The garden was so big that it made the house seem small, although it was, in truth, a fair-sized farm cottage, with thick stone walls and a roof coming down low above the small windows.

The girl who had spoken to him, and who had just got up from kneeling over the crocus bed, was probably about a year younger than he, but short and sturdy, with brown hair cut square across her forehead. She looked Hugh over carefully but not rudely. He was to learn that Hilda Storrs was rather slow and careful about everything she thought of doing, but that she acted very promptly once she had made up her mind. She had decided, now, just what should be done.

"The kite will surely catch somewhere. So I will go down to the gate and ask every person who comes past if he has seen it. And you had better go inside to my mother; she would like to give you some breakfast."

A pleasant woman with bright, dark eyes, who came out on the step at that moment, smiled her approval of Hilda's instructions and brought Hugh inside. There was, indeed, after all that running, a great hollow inside him where breakfast should have been. "You shouldn't take so much trouble," he protested politely, but was very glad, just the same, when she put a pan on the fire and began turning the hissing slices of bacon. The cottage inside was just what he would have expected, with its low ceilings, its bright-curtained windows and its stone floor scrubbed as white as any marble pavement could have been. She laid his breakfast and said little to him until he had finished.

"I think I know who you are," she observed then. "Your mother and I, when we were girls, used to go to the village school together. I wish you would tell her that Betsy Storrs sends her regards and would be glad to do anything for her that might be possible. We are all rejoiced that she and you have come here to live."

"You have a very beautiful garden," Hugh said, looking out through the window at the drifts of yellow below the wall.

"Yes, things are doing well. We raise flowers for the market in Philadelphia, and we grow vegetables in the fields beyond. My husband and Hilda and I try to take all the care of them, since my three older boys have gone away to work elsewhere."

At that moment Hilda came running in. "Sam, the carter, saw your kite, with the cord tangled in a tree, but still flying. It is inside Mr. Bonaparte's gates; he saw it over the wall."

"Which way?" asked Hugh, jumping up and seizing his cap.

"Down our lane and turn to the left when you get to the high road. There are big posts and iron gates when you get to Mr. Bonaparte's place; there is no other like it."

He got out a hasty thanks and was off down the lane. The kite was still flying—that was good. Presently he began to realize that it would be a long way and that he had better not try to run the whole of it, for even when he came to the high road there was a long stretch before him and Mr. Bonaparte's place not yet in sight.

The road was muddy, and the grass beside it long and wet. But white flowers were opening in the shelter of the hedges and there were the leaves of violets everywhere. Hugh liked flowers. Through one long spring, when he had been having measles and could not use his eyes in school, he had helped the gardener on a neighbor's estate and loved the feeling of making things grow. But he had never before seen flowers grown to be sold as they were at Hilda's house. It must be a pleasant way of making one's living, probably no real work at all. The wind had fallen and was no more, now, than a fresh breeze. The sun was out and the clouds were rolling up into high, towering masses of white, visible afar over the open country. It was good to see such distances, with no close-built villages to cut off the view. The air was clear and brightly warm. He liked America.

He was surprised to hear a call, "Hugh, Hugh," beyond the hedge. His brother Jeremy suddenly appeared, riding a fat gray horse and coming through a gap. "Mother and Grandfather wondered where you had gone, and Grandfather told me to take Dolly, the only horse he has left in the stable, and ride after you and the kite. I saw it as I came across the field; we ought to be able to get it back. Get up and ride and I will walk for a while. I want to find out how America feels under one's feet."

"It feels good," Hugh told him earnestly, and added, "The kite is at Mr. Bonaparte's place."

He was feeling something in his mind, trying to remember something. Where had he just heard Mr. Bonaparte's name before Hilda spoke it? To be sure, it was what people called the great Emperor of France when they wanted to make a joke—but then they did not make jokes about Napoleon now. No, it was someone else—oh, it was the gentleman in the chaise. "You're from France, eh? Then you'd better go down the road and call on Mr. Bonaparte."

They had arrived at a big open gate, and a driveway curving in between the high stone posts. There was a little cottage for a gatehouse, but at that moment there was no one in it to say whether they should enter or not. They went in.

A large white house was visible, but it was a great distance off. They could catch a glimpse of the kite, riding high, caught among the trees beyond it. The curve of the drive brought them to a broad stretch of lawn, and at the center of it a group of men, all occupied in the task of cutting down a beech tree. Two burly workmen with their coats off were chopping at the trunk and two more, who might be gardeners, were standing close by. At a little distance, watching with great interest, were two other figures, a slim, dark gentleman in a green coat and, beside him, a short man, his coat mulberry color, his waistcoat very fine, the tied ends of his stock very long. The others kept glancing round at him or asking him for directions; it was evident that he was the owner.

Hugh dismounted, and they left Dolly standing in the driveway as they walked across to ask permission to go farther. But no one paid any attention to them; all were watching intently, as people do when a tree is about to fall. The short man suddenly raised his voice, speaking in rapid French:

"No, no, wait. I have changed my mind. Make the tree fall the other way." With more speed than anyone could have expected, he dashed across the grass to make his order clearer to the men. But even as he moved, the tree gave that terrible crack which is the first sound of its falling.

It was Hugh and Jeremy alone who were not frozen at the sight of his danger, at the thought that a cry might stop him and make the risk worse than if he went on. But those two leaped forward, each catching him by an arm and dragging him backward as the tree came down. It crashed heavily, stabbed its branches into the soft earth and sent a shower of bark and twigs pattering down around them.

The short gentlemen uttered an exclamation in French,

looked at the two in wonder, but spoke at once to the man in the blue coat, who had come running up. "But I told them, Mailliard, that I wanted the tree to fall the other way."

Even Hugh knew more of the matter than he did, and blurted out, "Why, they could not change after they had chopped—"

"Hush," said the man who had been called Mailliard. He put a hand on Jeremy's arm and drew the two boys aside. "Do you not know to whom you are talking?"

"No—" began Jeremy, then taking another glance at the short man's face and figure, he exclaimed, "Why, he looks like—"

"Oh, peace, do not speak so loud," Mailliard warned them, dropping his voice. "Yes, you are right, he looks like the great Emperor Napoleon. That is because he is Napoleon's brother. He is Joseph Bonaparte, once King of Spain, now fled from his enemies and living for a time in America. He will want me to offer you his thanks. Perhaps there was no one of us who felt like laying hands on a man whom we are used to thinking of as a king. Now will you tell me how you came here? Oh, it was for the kite? Yes, fetch it if you wish. I was about to have Jules, the gardener, take it down."

The kite was caught to a big oak tree behind the house. Hugh had to climb on Jeremy's shoulders to get up into the branches, but he came down again carrying the kite safe and whole. Jules, the chief gardener, came to stand and watch from below, a little man with a network of a million dry wrinkles over his weather-beaten face. "I am glad you got it safely—it is a fine kite." He spoke in French. "And may one ask where you live?"

Jeremy told him. "With Mr. Hiram Nicolls, up on the ridge yonder."

"With Mr. Nicolls? Oh, then run quickly. There is a man in the driveway, just asking the shortest way to Mr. Nicolls' house, and we did not know what to tell him."

Just beyond where the boys had left Dolly standing in the road, a post chaise was drawn up, the same one which Hugh had met in the lane. The round-faced gentleman was standing on the grass, talking to Mr. Mailliard, Mr. Bonaparte's secretary. "I heard the crash of the tree," he was saying, "and just turned in to see if anything were wrong." He was a talkative fellow and in no hurry to go on about his errand, which he presently explained. "I have not been in this neighborhood before. Mr. Stephen Girard of Philadelphia sent me out to buy grain. And I have another errand too, a less pleasant one, for I have to carry bad news to Mr. Girard's friend Mr. Hiram Nicolls. Yes, I fear it's very bad news indeed."

If the gentleman of the post chaise had expected to ask directions from the two boys, he was disappointed, for the two of them were suddenly off down the driveway, Jeremy on the horse, Hugh hurrying alongside. "We can take a short way, up through the meadows the way I came down," Jeremy said. "We have to get there first. Grandfather shouldn't hear, without warning—whatever it is he had to be told."

"And Jackson—" Hugh added. Jackson with his pistol and his silly hope that he could keep evil tidings away by means of it—who knew what trouble that would lead to? Yes, they must get there first.

They crossed the large field and mounted a long gentle slope. As they looked back, they could see the chaise just rolling out of Mr. Bonaparte's gates and proceeding at an unhurried pace along the road. Hugh ran up the rise, while Jeremy took the horse along the hedge to find a gate. They looked back again and could see the moving body of the chaise swinging into the lane below. With all the strength that was in them, they pressed on.

The sun was so warm that Grandfather and the boys' mother had come out to sit on the stone bench at the edge of the terrace. They looked up, both startled, as the two came running across the grass to them. "Why, what is this?" Grandfather asked.

Now that they were there, it was hard to say what they had intended. But perhaps Jeremy had been preparing the words as he came. "You know, Grandfather, you have been here by yourself for a long time. But now you are not alone anymore. We are with you. We are here to help you, if we can, to help you no matter what may come."

Grandfather looked at him, but no longer in wonder. His thin cheeks had a little flush and his eyes lit with a spark under his deep eyebrows. "Yes?" he said. "And what is coming, then?"

"A man is coming, a stout man in a chaise. He has a message for you from Mr. Stephen Girard. And the message is bad news."

"Yes," said Grandfather again. "And I can tell you, even

before he arrives, what that message is. He will tell me that my ship, the Wanderer, is lost. She has been long overdue, I have been most anxious, and Mr. Girard was to send me word the moment he had certain tidings. And to know that she is lost means only one thing. It means that I am ruined."

He said it easily, almost lightly, but the drawn look upon his face told how deep and important was the truth. "That is what the kind, chattering man, Mr. James Anthony, will have to tell me. Well, let him come."

CHAPTER 2

Stephen Girard, Mariner and Merchant

When their grandfather mentioned the name of the man coming in the post chaise, Jeremy and Hugh suddenly came to themselves. They had warned Mr. Hiram Nicolls of the news that was coming, but there was something else of which to think. They ran across the garden and flung open the door of the kitchen but, with Jeremy setting the example, they walked in quietly enough. With an air of its being purely by chance, Jeremy put his shoulders against the door of the cupboard, and stood there easily, while Hugh spoke.

"Mr. James Anthony is coming in at the gate," he said.

Jackson's face brightened. "Why, it's long since we've had guests here, and the master will be wanting me to bring him out a glass of wine and a plate of biscuits," he said, but Nannie interrupted.

"Now, then, don't you see that it's him that's bringing the news we dreaded? Are you going to let him come in?"

"You can't help his coming in," Jeremy said steadily. "And Grandfather knows, without being told. He has really known before any of the rest of us. That kind of thing is not to be kept away with a pistol. But no one is to be frightened. We—we will think of something to do. This isn't the end."

"Why, sure, bless you, maybe after all it isn't the last thing to happen to all of us. Though that was what we dreaded, ever since we heard it through the gossip of seafaring men, that the master's last ship had gone down." Nannie was wiping her eyes with her apron, but her face was crinkling into smiles. "How the young do bring hope into a house. Yes, Mr. Nicolls will be wanting something for his visitor, and the silver tray is as black as your breeches."

Therefore, twenty minutes later, Jackson was handing a tray of refreshments to the guest, even though his intention had been to put a pistol to his head. Mr. James Anthony, quite unconscious of his narrow escape, was sitting on the bench beside of Hiram Nicolls, chattering cheerfully, relieved that the bad news he had brought had been so courageously received. After he had gone, however, the family gathered in serious council. It was then that, for a moment, Grandfather's spirit faltered.

"I had been begging you to come home to me, thinking always that I could win back to prosperity again. It was while you were at sea that this last disaster came. Through the years when the wars of Napoleon were everywhere, on sea and on land, the dangers of shipping were great, although the profits were also great. Two of my ships were captured by the British, three were seized in Danish ports on the grounds that they were carrying forbidden goods, although the truth was that they were not. I had one vessel left, the Wanderer; with her I could have built up a new trade, now that good times have come again. But she is wrecked off the Windward Islands in the West Indies, and I have nothing with which to go on. You have come home to me and I have nothing to give you." He stopped, and sat looking straight before him, down the slope across open country. His dark eyes were not even dim, but they knew that his heart was near to breaking. The boys' mother was the first to speak.

"We have very little ourselves, but there is no need for you to think of what you can give us. We are going to help to take care of you. We are going to find a smaller place to live that is not big and empty and cold. And there I am going to wait on you and make you comfortable and happy. That is the first thing."

"And I am going to find work." Jeremy was ready with his answer too. "There are a hundred things you can do when you are seventeen." He spoke with more confidence than, perhaps, he really felt, for seventeen is not, actually, so very old for starting out in a strange country. But Hugh had an idea and had no hesitations. "Mother, you say we should live in a smaller place? I know just where to go, and it is not far off."

Three days later the two Armond brothers were making another journey by water, not so long a one, this time, as the voyage from France. They were traveling from Bordertown to Philadelphia and, since the roads were muddy and horses not plentiful, they were going by the market boat that carried the Storrs family and all that they were taking to Philadelphia to sell.

The move to the Storrs' house had been made promptly, and the white house on the hill was closed. Nannie and Jackson had gone to stay with their married granddaughter, which, in fact, they had been longing to do, but had felt that they could not leave good Mr. Nicolls. Betsy Storrs and her husband John, a long quiet man, had welcomed them all warmly. These friendly lodgers would fill up the space left by the going away of the three sons. They had four tiny rooms up under the roof, one each for Grandfather and Eleanor Armond, one for the boys, and a fourth, arranged especially for Grandfather as a little sitting room that looked into the treetops and across the garden. Here Grandfather had most of his meals, often served by Hilda. She loved to carry them up and to stand across the table from him, talking earnestly. Hilda was excellent company when she could put her shyness behind her. And now, since all this was settled, Jeremy was setting out for Philadelphia to talk over Grandfather's affairs with Mr. Stephen Girard, and to discover whether something could be done.

The boys' mother had talked of coming, but at the last minute decided that Grandfather needed her presence. "You can ask Mr. Girard's advice as well as I can," she said. "Anything that he arranges I know would have my approval. I hope so much he can find some work for you."

Grandfather nodded. "Yes, if he has any plan, I am willing to agree to it. You could not ask a wiser or a kinder man."

No single cart could carry all that the Storrs family had to take to market at one time, so they had fallen into the habit of taking the load down the Delaware by boat. They went at night, so that the flowers and vegetables would be fresh for the early-morning market in the city streets. All of them slept as best they could in the afternoon, then, just as it was getting dusk, they carried down to the boat the daffodils in their buckets of water, the baskets of early vegetables, the violets, lettuce, chickens and cheeses. By the light of lanterns they got them aboard, packed so close that there was hardly room for people to move, with the smell of narcissus and freesias going up in the soft night air in an almost visible cloud of sweetness. Some hours later they crowded themselves in, rowed out into the current and set the big square sail. Other boats slipped out from the shore in the darkness, lights moved across the water, the smell of flowers was everywhere. Voices called from boat to boat. The stars were very bright overhead; the shores were ghostly as the boats slipped by.

Hugh was very still in his place in the bow. He had time to think now after the rush and hurry of the last few days. He wondered what Mr. Stephen Girard would be like; it was hard to guess. Mr. Girard had been a friend of Grandfather's since as long ago as when Mother was a little girl. He was a Frenchman, but had lived long in Philadelphia and had come to great prosperity there, by just the same sort of ventures of buying and selling as had ruined Grandfather. Fortune in war was an unaccountable thing. He would certainly be willing to help them. Would he help Hugh with the plan that he had? It was for reasons of his own that Hugh had asked that he might go with Jeremy to Philadelphia.

The lights of towns showed now and then, twinkling on one side of the river or the other. At first the boat went between ridges so that only the wooded banks were visible, then the shore, especially on the New Jersey side, rolled away to broad meadows, all so peacefully asleep, with a dim light here and there to show a house, or the faint shapes of cows and horses to be seen, grazing on the dewy grass. No one knew that they were passing; certainly no one knew that he, Hugh Armond, was traveling by, on the winding river, to seek his fortune. That was what Hugh felt sure that he was doing. And no one knew; no one knew. The broad bow, with an extra coat spread on it, was a comfortable place for him to curl up and try to sleep, with his eyes just above the gunwale, watching the shore slipping past. He did not watch it for long but fell deeply asleep. Jeremy and John Storrs had been taking turns at keeping awake to tend the big sail and hold the tiller. Back in the stern Hilda was asleep against her mother's shoulder. Hugh waked for a moment to see the sky turning white, with no color as yet; he lay watching as the day began to come, as the groups of houses clustered at the water's edge came into view. A voice cried across the water, "Bid you good morrow!" They had reached Philadelphia.

They all went to the inn at the waterside to rest a little, to eat breakfast and make themselves tidy. The big room was full of quiet, bright-faced people, even though the sun was only just showing over the housetops. They were all farming folk who had come with their wares to market, and the stands were being filled up all along the middle of Market Street. Everything was gay with color, with bright tulips, the orange or purple globes of cheese, the braided

wreaths of onions and dried red peppers. At the Storrs'
stall things were hardly in place before a lady in a flowered
bonnet, with a bright shawl trailing over her arms and with
a servant behind her carrying a basket, had stopped to
make the first purchase.

Hugh and Jeremy were discussing how soon they could
go to ask for Mr. Girard at his office in Water Street. Hilda
was sure that if they waited where they were they would
see him pass. "He likes to come to do his own marketing.
You can always tell whether he is going to have guests and
how grand the dinner is going to be by what he chooses,
especially the flowers."

People came and went, argued and bargained. Finally
Hilda whispered, "There he is." Hugh felt a little tremor go
over him. How much was going to depend on half an hour
of talk with Mr. Girard, on whether he could or would
understand what they wanted to tell him.

Like all the others Mr. Girard had a servant behind
him with a basket. He himself was well dressed, with the
dash of smartness that anyone with French blood almost
always has, but with nothing too noticeably fine about his
dark-blue coat and the watch chain and seals that crossed
his waistcoat. He had a high forehead, showing some
baldness, and a face that was keen, wise, kind and always
half smiling. One of his eyelids drooped, for he had no
sight in that eye. After a first glance no one would think
about that again, for the expression of his face was so
unusual, so gay and yet so intent.

He chose a great quantity of flowers to put in the
servant's basket, delicate white ones with a dash of

scarlet tulips. "My guests tonight are the new Spanish Ambassador and his suite," he told Hilda, with whom he seemed to be on the best of terms. "He is to land at our wharf this morning, for his ship is even now in the Delaware. I think these tulips are the color to catch his fancy."

While he spoke, he cast a shrewd, quick glance at the boys. Betsy Storrs presented them. "These are Mr. Jeremy and Mr. Hugh Armond, just come from France to the house of their grandfather, Mr. Hiram Nicolls."

Jeremy added, "It was my grandfather's wish that we talk over some of his affairs with you, since he could not come himself." And he said at the end, desperately, "I hope so that something can be done, sir."

"I think there is always something to be done," Stephen Girard answered.

He had finished his marketing so that they walked on together, while he asked a few questions. "I had been hoping that Hiram Nicolls would come to me himself or send a messenger," he told them. "Here is my counting room. We will go in."

Inside his office door were rows of tall desks with clerks standing at them, busy with papers and great account books. Mr. Girard led the boys into his inner room, where the view from the windows was of rows of wharves, of ships at the docks and men hustling back and forth with sacks and boxes and barrels. Above the desk was a picture of a ship, as was the portrait of some great lady. They all sat down. There was no need for explanations. Mr. Girard plunged at once into the heart of their grandfather's affairs.

"Every merchant loses some ships," he declared, "and in times of war he loses them in many ways. Some of your grandfather's are gone to the bottom forever, but there are three, still held in the harbor of Copenhagen, as he may have told you, seized on the charge that they carried unlawful goods. Two of mine were taken in the same way. Neither of us had broken the law, but under the orders of Napoleon Bonaparte many ships were seized thus in the hope of destroying trade with England. To get back our vessels, or the value of them, it is necessary to bring up a case in the law courts of Denmark. But that is a long process, almost impossible to carry through by letters. I have my own agent, Thomas Greening, at work upon it, and have made claims both for my ships and those of Hiram Nicholls. But there is more work in the matter than one man can attend to. Now if Hiram Nicolls could send someone thither to act on his behalf—" He stopped with his hand clasped round his long chin and looked across at Jeremy. "How old are you?" he asked abruptly.

Hugh saw his brother flush, half get up from his chair and then sit down again. "I am seventeen, sir," Jeremy told him.

"Seventeen! That is not as old as I could have wished. But none the less you could be of great help to Thomas Greening. I could find you a place as clerk on one of my ships, that would give you your passage over—" He spoke as though he were thinking aloud, as though arranging the simplest thing in the world.

"But—but, sir," exclaimed Jeremy, "do you mean that you think that I—I would be the person to go to Denmark to work for getting back my grandfather's ships?"

"Of course, that is what I mean," returned Girard. "The only thing that is not in convenient accordance with our plan is that you would need to get your mother's or grandfather's consent, and I have a ship, the Superb, sailing today, at the turning of the tide. It would be so fortunate if you could go in her."

Jeremy's face was pale, and Hugh's eyes were steadily on him. "My mother and my grandfather both said they would approve any plan of yours, sir," Jeremy said.

"Then," answered Stephen Girard boldly, "why delay? Many a voyage is settled as quickly as that. Young Hugh, when you return to Bordentown and tell your mother that I have sent your brother overseas, she will say but one thing, that he had no shirts or pocket handkerchiefs to take with him. So you, sir, go and buy him what he will need to use at once; later his clothes can be sent to him from home. Here is money, for I undertake to advance all the expenses of the voyage. It will all return to me in the end. Come back in an hour, and meanwhile I will be giving your brother some instructions."

Hugh went out, leaving the two with their heads bent over the papers on the desk. He came back at the end of the appointed time, carrying the canvas duffle bag which, with Betsy Storrs' help, he had bought and filled. Her own second son was a sailor, so that she knew what to advise. The two at the desk were still deep in talk. "You understand that I take full responsibility for sending you to Denmark in such haste," Mr. Girard was saying. "It is of the greatest importance that you join Mr. Greening while he is still in England. Your brother will explain all that when he goes home."

One of the clerks rapped at the door and spoke respectfully. "The Infanta Maria, the Spanish ship, is even now warping in to the wharf, sir. She has come up the river with the very last of the tide. The Superb will be sailing in no more than a few minutes."

There was a bustle of gathering things together for Jeremy, letters that had been written for him to carry, money in a little bag. In the midst of it Stephen Girard suddenly bent his cordial smile on Hugh. "This is leaving you a little out of things, my dear sir, but you and I must make better acquaintance," he said. "You go down to the wharf with your brother, while I make my polite addresses to the Spanish Ambassador. But after that I am free, and should like you to eat lunch with me, here in this room. But now you must both make haste."

Hugh would indeed have felt lost and forlorn without those friendly words. He shouldered the duffle bag; Jeremy pocketed the letters and the little bag of gold. Mr. Girard shook him by the hand and they went out. The clerk gave them directions.

"Go to the very last wharf, almost a quarter of a mile down. The Superb is already anchored out in the channel, waiting for the tide. Get a man to signal and they will send a boat for you. But you have precious little time, for the Captain does not know you are coming and may get under way without you."

The street along the water front was full of sunshine, of stir and bustle and crowded with people. For a moment they wondered why, then saw above the roofs of the warehouses the great towering masts and drooping furled sails of a huge ship. This was the Infanta Maria, greatest vessel of the Spanish Navy, sent to bear their Ambassador to America in proper state and landing at Philadelphia as being the port most convenient to Washington. A throng of people had turned out to see the ship come in, an excited crowd which grew thicker and thicker, with everyone pushing to get a good view of the splendid vessel as she swung in. Hugh and Jeremy dodged this way and that; they pushed between elbows and ducked around shoulders. The need for haste was desperate. Could they possibly make it? Hugh, with the advantage of being smaller, darted here and squeezed through there; he did not stop an instant to stare up at the great ship. Jeremy came pushing behind. They had got through somehow; they could see the Superb riding at anchor, her sails going up one by one. Jeremy spoke breathlessly to one of the dockmen. "Mr. Girard said you were to signal for me." For a moment the boys thought they were too late; but no, a boat was swung out and was lowered into the water and was rowed briskly toward them.

Jeremy and Hugh stood silent, watching it come. It was the first moment, now, that they had time to think what was really going to happen. Hugh turned to stare at Jeremy as though he were impressing on his mind in one last glance his thin figure, his dark blue eyes with black lashes, his dark hair. Jeremy looked down at his sturdy young brother whose blue eyes devoured his face in their turn.

"How—how long do you think it may be?" Hugh asked

in a voice that hardly sounded like his own.

"I never thought." Jeremy calculated for a second. "Two months—that would be only enough to get to Denmark; two more. Six anyway, I will be gone, Hugh. It might even be a year." Hugh's throat suddenly felt very tight, and he could not say anything. Jeremy went on steadily. "You will have to take care of them. You must do what you can."

"I have thought of something to do. I am going to talk to Mr. Girard about it when we have lunch together." The boat had come to the foot of the ladder now. It was time. There was a very abrupt goodbye, then Jeremy was in the stern of the boat, moving out across the water. The tide was just turning, the Superb was swinging round. Jeremy was over the side; he was waving from the deck.

There was no need for breathless haste now. Hugh could stand as long as he wanted, watching her get up her last sails and slide past the point, seeming to grow slimmer and taller as she moved into the distance. The great bend of the river swallowed her, little now, and moving out of sight. He drew a great long breath and turned away.

Hugh felt greatly refreshed and cheered again as he sat at lunch with Mr. Stephen Girard in his private office. The fish with its rosettes of potatoes and vegetables, and the long loaf of crusty bread all reminded him of France and told him that Mr. Girard's cook was a Frenchman. He had something to ask Mr. Girard, but he would wait a little— this was not quite the time yet. The lunch was passing, the man who waited on them set down the dessert of French pastry. Hugh must begin now, but he could not find the words. Suppose Mr. Girard would laugh at him? Mr.

Girard rather abruptly broke off what he was saying to ask a question.

"Did you ever see Napoleon?"

"Yes," Hugh answered. "I saw him once. I can never forget it. And I think—yes, I do remember, there was another time, when I was very little."

He went back in his mind to make sure. All through the time when Hugh was very young, people had talked of Napoleon, the greatest man in France, then the greatest man in Europe—in all the world. He was head of the New French Republic; then, all of a sudden, he was Emperor. He had made France very great and glorious, people said. But presently they began to say, "It is good to be so glorious, but why are we always at war?" They had begun to be very tired of war. But it was in those days that Hugh had seen him first, one day in Paris, marching at the head of his soldiers up the great Avenue of the Champs Elysées. First came flags and music, then the one man riding alone on his white horse. Everyone knew that he was a little man, but he did not look little now, as he bowed his head and the people screamed and shouted and waved their hats and cheered again until it seemed that the buildings would rock behind them. Then came the soldiers, marching by in an unending flood. The rumble of their tramping feet was an even greater sound than the cheering, a sound to be remembered longer. Hugh was so small then that his father had to take him on his shoulder so that he could see over the crowd. That was the first time he saw Napoleon. He sometimes wondered whether he had really seen all that, or only remembered hearing Jeremy talk of it. But yes, he must have seen it; otherwise he could not have remembered so clearly the sound of the soldiers' feet.

But there was no chance of his forgetting the second time. He knew that Napoleon's good fortune had come to an end, that he was beaten in war at last and was sent to the Island of Elba in the Mediterranean, so that he could no longer rule France. Hugh remembered how his father had arranged so hurriedly that their mother and Jeremy and Hugh should leave France for England, how the three of them had journeyed so hastily across the channel and that after they had landed they heard that Napoleon had come back and that there was fighting again. Their mother was anxious about their father, left behind in Paris and not well. They waited and waited for news. It came at last. Napoleon had lost everything, he was fleeing from his enemies, the fighting was over. Their mother at once set about going home to their father; it was not easy to get passage, but a little ship which was going to Bordeaux would take them. They had been some time out and were far beyond the sight of light, when, early one morning almost before daylight, Jeremy was shaking Hugh by the shoulder, telling him to wake, to wake quickly. Hugh stumbled on deck and wondered first why he had been called. They were passing a British vessel, a warship with tall masts and a vast spread of sail, but what was that to cause such excitement; they had all seen warships before.

Their little vessel tacked near, and Hugh shivered in the cold of the early morning as he and Jeremy looked up and saw that face at the rail above the warship's tall side. It was a pale face, determined, quiet. There were the high forehead and the dark hair across it, the firm countenance, the square shoulders, the uniform. It was Napoleon, Emperor no longer, surrendered to his enemies, being carried away to that far island of St. Helena in the South Atlantic, where, this time, he would be beyond the reach of any hope of escape. He did not see them. He was looking across the water to where the shores of France should be. They were out of sight, but he saw them in his heart, no person could doubt that—the waves on the beach, the green hills, the clustering houses, the châteaux, the palaces, the great city of Paris, so quiet now, with no waving flags, no music of a triumphing army. For him the rumble of marching feet had ceased forever. Yes, Hugh had seen Napoleon. He told Mr. Girard of it, of both times.

His friend sat listening intently, his eyes on the tablecloth. He spoke when Hugh had finished his account. "Every man of French blood has thought of little except Napoleon for all these years. I loved the French Republic. I was proud of Napoleon when he was at its head. I feared when he became Emperor; I feared still more when the glories of France became so great through his wars that they were bound to give way. And, like all Frenchmen, when the end came, I was moved to pity for Napoleon, over his fall from so high a place. But I can see the truth about him more clearly through having become a citizen of these free United States. I left France when I was not much older than your brother Jeremy. I did not go back to it— why? Because I was ruined, Monsieur Hugh, ruined and in debt, in worse case even than your good grandfather. But I was young—that was my advantage—and out of ruin a man can build up fortune again, can pay his debts and even, with good luck, can manage to be of some help to another who has lost all." He pushed back his chair; the lunch was over. Hugh must ask his question now.

"Do you think, sir," he began, "that, now that Jeremy is gone, I might manage to do something too? I should earn something, for Mother has little money and Grandfather has none. I know about gardening; I helped a gardener once for two months. And there is a big garden near us, that belongs to an odd gentlemen—" Was Mr. Girard going to ask him, also, how old he was? When he said twelve, would it make the whole idea seem ridiculous? He could not go on.

"An odd gentleman called Joseph Bonaparte," Mr. Girard said for him. "Brother of the Emperor, as you have no doubt heard, once King of Spain, once King of Naples, ambassador, and all such things, even a general—when he had to be. And you would like to work as helper to the gardener of Mr. Bonaparte? That, I would say, is the best of ideas. You are a proper size for a gardener's boy and, I am led to guess, would be a good one. But tell me this, how about your going to school?"

Hugh was glowing with delight. Mr. Stephen Girard really approved of his plan. And as for school . . . "I was going to school up to the very day we sailed for America," he urged. "And now it is nearly April. It will soon be May. American schools end in June, Hilda says. Do you think I need to go, just for that little time?"

"No," agreed Mr. Girard. "To come from studying in France would make it a little difficult to fit into the school at Bordentown, and had better be done at the beginning of

a term. They like to employ people who can talk French at
Point Breeze—that is the name of Mr. Bonaparte's estate.
Old Jules Renard, the chief gardener, will be delighted. He
is, above all things, a gossip, and only his great devotion
to the family of Bonaparte keeps him in a country where
he cannot know the affairs of every household within ten
miles round about him. Mr. Bonaparte has asked for my
advice about many things, so that he will be glad to listen
to any recommendation that I make. I will write a letter
to Mr. Bonaparte, which you can give to his secretary, Mr.
Mailliard."

Hugh got up, wondered how in the world he could
thank him, began to try. Stephen Girard cut him short.
"You are to say nothing of that. But I bid you remember
this. I am recommending not just a gardener's boy, but a
friend, the son and the grandson of a friend. I give you this
last instruction. Keep your eyes and your ears well open,
my dear friend Hugh, say little, but watch always. Strange
things can happen in the household of a man who has
been a king, and who is the loyal brother of that person
who has been sent into exile as the highest enemy of all
Europe. Some day—it will not be soon—but some day Mr.
Bonaparte, hearing that you have lived in France, will ask
you, as I have, 'Did you ever see Napoleon?' Tell him of the
first time, but not of the second."

The Storrs family went back with the boat the next day
but saw Hugh off first on the early-morning coach, since
he was in haste to get back to Bordentown, and travel up
the Delaware was very slow. But in spite of his hurry, he
stopped the coach two miles south of the lane that led to

the Storrs cottage, and had himself set down at the great iron gates of the estate of Point Breeze. He wondered what the people on the coach, who sat about him so unnoticing, would have thought if he had said, in clear tones so that they all could hear:

"I wish to get down here, for I have a letter in my pocket to give to Mr. Bonaparte, the brother of the Emperor Napoleon." Of course, he did not say it. But he climbed down and walked through the gate as the coach rolled away. He would have a great piece of news to announce when he got home, about Jeremy and his voyage to England and Denmark. But he intended to have another also, about himself and his employment as gardener's boy on the estate of Mr. Joseph Bonaparte.

CHAPTER 3

Mr. Bonaparte

Any kind of work is made happier by the good will and friendship of those who work together. Hugh thought many times that, if it had not been for Hilda, it might not have been possible for him to get, or to hold, the warm friendship of Jules Renard, the old Frenchman who was Mr. Bonaparte's chief gardener. Mr. Bonaparte did not read Stephen Girard's letter himself; that was attended to by his secretary Mr. Louis Mailliard. He glanced Hugh over with a faint look of having seen him before, but evidently did not recollect his having part in the incident of the falling tree. But for Jules Renard, with the puckering brown face and lean, wrinkled skillful hands—for him it was no effort to remember where they had met.

"So," he said, "you are to leave kite flying and seek employment here? And you speak French. For that I am thankful enough. You live in this neighborhood? Then perhaps—of course, it is of no importance— but perhaps you could tell me something of the sort of people who dwell round about. Are they good with poultry? Do they know how to trim their apple trees in spring?"

Hilda Storrs had managed to give Hugh a very great

amount of information about the neighbors and what they did. She was usually a silent little girl, but as Hugh helped her to weed the garden or churn the butter, she seemed moved to talk freely to him, more freely, even, than to Hugh's grandfather with whom she was such good friends. She seemed to feel that Hugh was something of a stranger in America, and that therefore he must learn as much as she could tell him so that he might feel more at home among them. Mr. Hansell, for instance, on the next farm, had been trying to start a flock of white turkeys, but they were so wild and ran away so much that any day you would meet one person or another, struggling down the road with a white turkey in a basket or under his arm, trying to return it to the Hansell farm. On the place beyond his, William Cummins had a pea patch which always bore early peas a whole week before anyone else had them ready, and nobody knew why. They saw him sometimes lighting fires on frosty nights, so that the clouds of warm smoke would drift over the rows, but no one else thought that was worth the trouble.

It was also Hilda's idea to ask Jules Renard to come on Sunday afternoon to drink tea at the Storrs' house, and to invite some neighbors—the two Risards, who had come from Rheims when they were children and could still talk French. How the old gardener's face broke into smiles when he was given that information.

"For two years I have spoken to no one except those on this estate alone," he declared. "And now I am to have friends among those who dwell round about. That goes well, that goes very well indeed." He was evidently most grateful to Mr. Girard for sending him such a useful gardener's boy.

There was a great deal of work, and there was much to learn and remember, even besides what had to do with planting and digging and watering.

"When any person of the household, Monsieur Mailliard, or Monsieur Bodine, the undersecretary, or when Monsieur Bonaparte himself goes by, you are to watch, and if his eye seems to light upon you, then you are to stand up and bow, most politely. I notice with pleasure that someone has taught you how to bow as a boy should. But if they do not take note of you, then go on with your work. If possible, you are to slip away, if you can do so without seeming to interfere with their movements, but if that cannot be done, just go quietly forward with what you are doing. Just remember that to grand gentlemen like those who surround Monsieur Bonaparte, the person of a gardener's boy, or even of a gardener, is as nothing, no more than a bush or a wheelbarrow." And he added, not without a trace of malice in his tone, "To Monsieur Bodine, the assistant secretary, we are as rather less than nothing. I see, with some dismay, my child, that you have already learned this abominable American habit of sometimes speaking before you are spoken to. That must not be; that must never be."

He went pottering about in his blue smock, touching the box cutting and the young shrubs as though with a magic hand, for everything he set out immediately fell to growing. The house had only just been finished; it was very large, the central part of wood, painted white, the wings of brick. The garden was to be very elaborate, but it was only begun. To Hugh's taste, it was sometimes a little queer to plant clumps of bushes and trees where there could be such wide sweeps of lawn, to make rustic summerhouses and set up statues and build flights of steps up and down, when the long slopes of the natural land, the drift of woods and open hillside would have been so much more beautiful. The whole estate opened on the edge of the hill above the Delaware, where it was joined by the steep ravine of Crosswicks Creek. There was a glorious view of twisting channels and wooded islands, at which he never tired of looking. It was between the house and the brow of the hill that the flower garden was to be laid out, a matter which he and Jules alone had to do, with little help from the large force of men which was at work sodding, leveling, laying out drives and building bridges across hollows over the whole estate.

At the end of seven days Hugh had begun to feel that he knew something of the place and of what was expected of him. He usually had a little free time in the middle of the day when Jules went into the house for a long, leisurely dinner in the servants' hall, with much talk and sipping of glasses of sugar and water and no haste over leaving the table. Hugh liked to spend it in a special spot of his own choosing, under the great oak tree which grew behind the house near the edge of the hill—the same one in which his kite had caught. Jules, who was very particular about such things, could not rest until he knew its exact name, since none of its kind grew outside America. John Storrs finally told him; it was a scarlet oak.

It was very big; there could be no doubt that Indians had sat under its branches to look out across the Delaware. There had been white settlers in this region many years before even Philadelphia was founded, and one of these had cleared away the smaller saplings from around it, so that it had grown to full height and compass of great branches without any crowding by lesser or meaner trees. In the Delaware valley, where the sunny days and the soft, dewy nights are unmatched in value for growing things, the trees are likely to reach notable height and glory. There were beech trees in the park, whose great branches drooped until their elbows lay on the ground, there were pines of commanding size, but, to Hugh's mind, there was no tree of them all so fine as this. This rose-colored cloud of early buds was giving place, now, to a green veil of opening leaves. The great black trunk had thrown out buttresses and high-shouldered roots, between two of which, in a deep hollow, he loved to lie and rest and think. He could look out over the river, and, in another direction, could see across the park, could even see his grandfather's house, far and white in the distance, set on its own ridge.

He was thinking, on that particular warm noontide, a hot day with a threat of April rain—thinking that he would be taking his first wages home that night. Hilda would be excited; his mother and his grandfather would be proud. It would mean the beginning of—what was it the beginning of? Hugh let his mind drift into the future, drift to Jeremy and the places he was seeing. And, suddenly—he could not at all say why—there went over him the thought, cold and terrifying, the wonder as to whether he could really endure it to go on with what he was doing.

It was all very well for a week, for a month, for any time that he himself chose. But to work on and on, to do things always by the orders of someone else, to have no time to himself except when he was tired with a long day's work, to be always weeding and watering and spading and seeing Mr. Bonaparte walk by, and Mr. Mailliard and Mr. François Bodine, the undersecretary, with the red hair and the haughtiest manner of them all—could he bear it? Was he going to bear it? His spade stood in the flower bed where he had been digging; his rake lay beside it. Suppose he took them and carried them very quietly over to the shed, and left them, just walked away and said nothing? A boy his mother had once hired had done that very thing—Hugh had looked out the window and had seen him stealing away. That boy was eleven; he was twelve. He had great reason for keeping on with his work; the work itself was of his own choosing. Yes, he must keep to it—but could he, could he?

It must have been a very sharp sound that called him back so abruptly to the green world where he lay in the hollow between the oak roots. The noise was not from the heavy footsteps of Jules, returning to his work, whistling a little as he stumped down the path. This sound was the sharp snapping of twigs, the rustle of thick bushes. Hugh raised his head a little, still sheltered by the great shoulder of the root.

He remembered now that he had seen, noticing it idly, a very small boat on the river, moving in toward shore. It was out of sight now; it must have come in to the bank and disappeared under the trees that covered the face of the bluff. And, it was plain, someone had landed and come up the hill, not by the open path, but in a straight line, moving behind the cover of the bushes and tree trunks. Hugh lifted his head a little higher, to look better.

A man was peering out from a clump of rhododendrons, a man with dark hair and so white a face that his eyes looked sharp and black under the line of his black eyebrows. He was turning his head and looking carefully this way and that; he seemed in no hurry to move out into the open. Hugh saw his eyes follow the long line of windows across the back of the house, as though he were counting them. The man craned his neck and peered far to the right and left, taking in every detail of the building. Was he hesitating, trying to make out the proper door for a stranger to approach with some more or less humble errand to this great house? No, for after long and careful examination, he turned about as though he had seen enough, and began to walk away down the hill. Hugh was thinking quickly, wondering. Was it anything unusual for a stranger to be examining the place where lived a man who had once been a king? No, it was not. And yet the man's actions were strange. Hugh came to his decision suddenly. It would not do to let him get away without asking him what he wanted. He jumped up and ran after him.

The fellow had got part way down the slope before he looked up and saw Hugh crashing through the bushes behind him. Surprisingly, he took to his heels and ran, ran as though his very life depended on getting back to his boat before Hugh could catch up with him. Without stopping to think, without even calling out, Hugh hastened the faster. He tripped over a root and plunged forward, not quite losing his balance but going down in the great strides and jumps that were necessary to keep him upright. It was so that he caught up with the stranger, crashed into him with a force that made them both fall, so that they rolled over and over, sometimes together, sometimes apart, Hugh struggling to catch the fellow's coat, the man jerking violently to keep himself free. He struck, missed Hugh, and then was in the water, splashing to push off his boat, climbing in over the side and picking up the oars.

There was nothing to be done now. Hugh stood on the bank and finally shouted the question that he should have asked at first. "What did you want? What were you doing?"

The fellow only settled to his oars and pulled as hard as he could down the river. The tide was with him, and he made good time. Then the rain, which had been threatening for the last hour, dropped suddenly between, first in a blur of big drops, then in the gray wall of a heavy downpour. Hugh turned about and went up the hill, finding himself thoroughly drenched before he got to the top. The man had not said a word. He did not look like an American. His sleeve was torn by a jutting branch and Hugh had caught a glimpse of the fine white fabric of his shirt. All that told very little. Hugh came to the top of the hill, wondering to whom he had better report this surprising thing that he had seen. Certainly someone in authority should know of it.

The garden was empty because of the rain, so he ran across the grass to the house. He should have gone to the door in the wing, the one for servants and messengers, but he was in too great haste, too excited to remember that. He went in at the main entrance and stood for a moment, bewildered, not knowing just where to go. The passageway from the garden door led into a central hall, very high, and paved with black and white marble. Doors in big arches opened from it in four directions. He hesitated, uncertain. Down one corridor he could see a great, stately room with tall arched windows and heavy curtains, with a vast chandelier hanging from the ceiling in a fairyland of crystal drops. But there was no one in sight. Mr. Mailliard, Mr. Bonaparte must still be at dinner.

The walls everywhere were hung with great pictures; there were paintings on the walls of the smaller rooms at both sides of the hall. He looked at one on the wall opposite him, a man on a horse with a storm breaking about him. That was Napoleon crossing the Alps. Hugh had seen that same picture when it was on show in Paris. And beyond an open door he saw a bust on a pedestal, the same face, dark bronze and very cold and stern and serious. That was Napoleon again. He looked about. Napoleon was everywhere.

A door opened and voices sounded in the hallway to the left. Mr. Bonaparte and Mr. Bodine were coming from the dining room, deep in talk. Hugh ran forward to speak to them.

"I saw such a strange thing, a man hiding in the bushes, looking so queerly at the house—"

Mr. Bodine interrupted him. "This is no place for you. This is no way in which to speak before His Excellency. If you have anything to say, you should send a proper message. And your feet—"

Hugh looked down, abashed. His feet were wet and had left tracks on the velvet carpet. He should have stayed on the marble. Bodine was saying to Mr. Bonaparte:

"It is the new gardener's boy. He knows nothing of how he should behave."

But Hugh was desperate, certain beyond anything that what he had seen meant something important. "But I had to tell you; I couldn't wait," he insisted. He looked pleadingly at Mr. Bonaparte, feeling sure that he must see how pressing the matter was.

But Mr. Bonaparte was stiff and offended, too, and actually did not know what to say. There among the pictures and statues of his famous brother he appeared to be only a fussy little man, getting stout, rather too full of his own importance. His voice was kind, but he too was refusing to listen.

"Bodine is right. That is not the way to speak either to him or to me." They both had overlooked the fact that Hugh spoke as good French as they, and so might possibly be not just the sort of gardener's boy they were taking him for. Bodine added a final word.

"Go down the passage past the kitchen and speak to Hamel, the major-domo, and if the matter seems really important, he will report to me what you have said. But there are a thousand strangers who come gaping about the house, hoping to catch sight of His Excellency so that they can say that they have seen a king. Do not let yourself be unduly excited over such small things, and never again come into His Excellency's presence in such fashion."

Hugh made his bow, of the sort that Jules approved so much, and went down the corridor toward that part of the house where workers belonged. He had tried his best; he could do no more. There was no use in trying to explain to anyone else. He knew well enough that this was no idle passer-by who wanted to look at the King of Spain, or at a house that was built like a palace.

He was boiling with wrath at the words of François Bodine. But as he came out into the garden, a sudden thought came to him. Mr. Girard had said that he was to keep his eyes and his ears open, that strange things could come about in such a house as this. Yes, this was one of the strange things. He would see Mr. Girard sometime and would tell him about it. Jules was waiting at the end of the path, trowel in hand.

"The rain came at just the right minute. Now the ground is perfect for moving the primroses. Take your spade."

It was the same spade which, not half an hour ago, Hugh had thought of taking quietly to the shed, to leave it there forever. But he had quite forgotten about that now.

After another week had passed and another, it seemed rather a matter of course that he should be working there. He could feel that what he earned was of real help in the household at home, where everyone had so very little, but where no one seemed to be at all unhappy as a result. The Storrs were untiringly kind; his mother was wise and careful in all her plans. The only thing they really wanted was letters from across the seas, and those could not be got with money, only with time. Time moved steadily, but very slowly.

Because he was not needed at a very early hour at
Point Breeze, he would often help with the work in the
Storrs' garden, where Hilda toiled as steadily as he. They
talked busily together as they worked along the borders,
with John Storrs showing them where to weed and doing
the heaviest part of the work. Hilda loved to have Hugh
tell her about the house at Point Breeze, especially of his
glimpse of the inside of it. Of the outside she had seen
a little herself for she had gone there with strawberries
and fresh butter. One of the maids had told her that in
Mr. Bonaparte's own bedroom was a bureau of a hundred
drawers! "Ties and shirts and waistcoats—enough to fill
them all!" the young woman had said.

Hilda sighed a little over the thought that she would
never have a chance to see all this for herself. "I love
beautiful houses," she would say longingly, but since not
even Hugh had a chance to see it all, there seemed to be no
hope that she should.

They talked of everything and anything; they began to
give each other instructions in history, Hugh explaining
what had happened in France, Hilda recounting the things
he did not know that had come about in America.

"Napoleon," he would begin, "was born on the Island of
Corsica, which is in the Mediterranean Sea. He lived in a
plain house, and he had many brothers and sisters. He had
no way of knowing that he would ever be ruler of France,
of half of Europe."

Hilda was an apt pupil. Presently her comment was, "He
did not know, either, that he would lose everything in the

wars at last and would be sent away to St. Helena. I wonder what he thinks there, Hugh. I wonder what he is thinking." But for that Hugh had no reply.

Then Hilda would begin in her turn. "William Penn came from England a very long time ago, to make a place where every kind of people could live in peace together. Pennsylvania was all his, and he brought Englishmen and Germans and Dutch here; they all worked hard and liked it. He built himself a house across the river from Bordentown, on the Pennsylvania side of the Delaware. The place was called Pennsbury. It was a big house, but not splendid and full of silk curtains and pictures and statues, like Mr. Bonaparte's. It was pulled down, but there are people who have seen it and can talk about it; they can tell how the Indians came to see him there and how everybody loved him."

She would tell him about George Washington also, more than Hugh had learned from his mother. It was hardly more than twenty years ago that Washington had lived in Philadelphia as President of the new United States, and had worked so hard for the government of his country, after he had fought such long years for her liberties. "My father and mother have both seen him; your grandfather knew him." Hugh talked to his grandfather about Washington. What he heard made him seem very near.

Hugh was working at Point Breeze one day, at the edge of the summerhouse, close to the angle of the hedge. It was very warm and still, one of the first days of May. He saw a rabbit skip through the hedge, and then presently caught sight of a slower-moving animal, low-hung and plump, which seemed to flow along the ground as it hurried forward on short legs. This was the groundhog whose burrow Hugh had found halfway down the hillside toward the river. He wondered a little why the creatures had left the shady thickets on the river bank and had come up into the garden. A sound of footsteps alarmed them, and they bustled away around the pedestal of a statue of Diana.

Mr. Bonaparte and Mr. Mailliard were coming down the path talking busily. Hugh stood up, not realizing that they could not catch sight of him from the point where they stopped for a minute, for he had seen them approaching and thought surely that they knew he was there. But suddenly Mr. Mailliard raised his voice to stress something that he was saying.

"Indeed, sir, at my age I have no real fancy for digging up buried jewels. I would that you could ask someone else."

"But it was you who chose the spot to bury them," Joseph Bonaparte answered.

This would not do, it would not do at all, Hugh thought. He must get away, for certainly they did not intend to be overheard. Jules had told him never to push his way past any gentleman of the household, so that he turned about to manage his escape through the hedge, crawling through a low gap on his hands and knees, making as little noise as he could. And it was so that he came face to face with the man who was listening.

The fellow was kneeling against a tree, bending forward, his dark face eager, the same man whom Hugh had seen spying on the place before. He saw Hugh, swung a vicious blow at him, but did not have a long enough reach. Once more he was off, fleet-footed, racing down the hill to his boat. That a grown man would run from a boy of twelve, run from him twice, meant certainly that there was something very much amiss. But Hugh did not pursue him this time. It was plain that the fellow was not going to linger in that neighborhood once he was discovered. Hugh stood watching him go and wondering what he should do. There was no use speaking to Mr. Bonaparte or Mr. Mailliard—he would never try that again. Mr. Mailliard was far kinder and more friendly than François Bodine, but still he might be offended, and so might Mr. Bonaparte. Jules had gone to the village so that he could not speak to him of the matter. He was not sure whether he should, even if he were there. But he might, perhaps, get from Jules some information that would cast light on Mr. Mailliard's strange remarks. He could do that without betraying any secrets overheard by chance.

The next day was Sunday, and Jules was invited for tea to the Storr's house. The whole family loved to have him come; even John Storrs liked to sit by, with his grave face quiet and intent, listening as Jules talked of France, and as Hugh translated to Hilda and her father. Jules had the gift, the valuable possession of many simple people, of telling all about everything and making every word sound interesting. Betsy Storrs could talk a little of his own tongue; she would settle him comfortably by the kitchen fire, telling him of this occurrence or that in the neighborhood, at which his face would beam brighter and brighter.

"So he has made up the quarrel with his cousin's

husband? Now, I thought it would be so—I knew it would be so," he would exclaim, entering into the matter as though he had known forever every person in that quarter of New Jersey.

Presently Eleanor Armond would come downstairs from where she had been reading to her father, and would sit down and talk to Jules. Then would his old face really shine, for she could talk to him of his own village in France; she had been in it and knew the very hillside where his grandfather's vineyard had been planted. She would sit in the big chair, bright-haired, friendly, dignified; and Hugh, sitting on the stool, or getting up to hand the teacakes, thought he had never seen anyone more quietly beautiful than his mother. Old Jules fairly worshipped her.

"I see you are well," he would say, "but I see also that you are a little anxious, waiting for news of that son who is beyond the seas. You have not heard from him yet? That is most disappointing, but the time will come presently. It is still too soon."

On that Sunday Hugh, instead of sitting by and repeating to John Storrs and Hilda what Jules was saying, pulled his stool close and took a hand in the talk himself. Jules loved to listen to gossip and also to repeat it, when urged a little. It was on that habit that Hugh was counting now.

"Monsieur Jules," the boy asked, thinking it was best to put a plain question, "are there jewels buried anywhere at Point Breeze?"

Everyone looked astonished—everyone except Jules.

"No, no," the old gardener answered. "The jewels are buried at Pranguins, the estate in Switzerland where Mr. Bonaparte was living before we came to America. My good master had fled from Spain, where the rascals would no longer have him for their king, not even at Napoleon's bidding, so he took refuge in Switzerland. The Emperor Napoleon had been sent to Elba where he was to stay and make no more war in Europe. But presently came the news that Napoleon had come back from Elba, and that he had gathered an army and was marching through France to take possession of his throne and his old power. Monsieur Joseph Bonaparte left in haste in the night to go to join him, but, before he went, he and Monsieur Mailliard gathered up the jewels and the gold ornaments that stood for so great riches and looked for a safe place to hide them. The part of the Chateau of Pranguins was full of fox holes, and it was in one of them that the box of gems was hidden. How do I know, child? I know because it was I who helped them dig. Such men as they are of little use at digging for themselves, I can tell you. Then there came the great battle of Waterloo, and once more Napoleon lost his power and all the family of Bonaparte must flee."

"And that was when Mr. Joseph Bonaparte came to America?" Eleanor Armond asked. Jules nodded.

"Yes, madame. Our Monsieur Joseph, he had found an American sea captain who would take him off in his ship and carry him safe to the United States. He went to his brother in the night and said to him that they were enough alike, that Napoleon should take his place and escape by sea, while Joseph remained to face his enemies.

But Napoleon was too proud; he said no, he would do nothing that looked like running away. He felt sure that he, an Emperor, would suffer no harm at the hands of fair men, even though he had fought against them and was now beaten. So he surrendered himself to the captain of a British ship. Then Monsieur Joseph, knowing that he could do no more, took his own way to America, and Napoleon was carried so far, so far away to St. Helena. But now things are quiet, and Monsieur Joseph grows a little short of money, so Monsieur Mailliard is to be sent to find the jewels and bring them back. But Monsieur Mailliard does not care so very much to go. Old servants like me know many things, and among friends like you it does no harm to speak of them."

"But is that all?" insisted Hugh. "Are there not jewels, or something of great value in the house, something that a crafty man would like to lay his hands upon, would like to steal?"

Everyone was quiet, waiting for the answer. An odd look came over Jules' face, a gleam of something secret, as well as something very obstinate. "Yes, there is something in that house that is more tempting for certain thieves even than jewels," he said. But after a little pause, he added, "Do you think old Jules Renard would tell of that? No, not he. That is a real secret. That is never to be told."

CHAPTER 4

A Letter from Overseas

The mail rider, who carried the letter bags from Philadelphia to Bordentown, came trotting up the drive at Point Breeze one sunny day at noon. He usually had so much mail for the Bonaparte house that he would rather leave it on his way than carry it to the post office in Bordentown. He nodded to Hugh, who was raking the gravel of the drive, and then pulled up. "It seems to me that I have a great thick letter from over yonder for you in my pouch, and that you might as well have it now. And there is a thinner one for you also; upon my word, it is from Stephen Girard. Everyone in Philadelphia knows that seal." He looked at Hugh with great respect, but grinned as he saw that the boy was unfolding the foreign letter first. "I had a brother at sea myself," he said. "I know what it is to wait and wait for letters."

Hugh scarcely remembered to thank him, but ran away to his place under the big oak tree—the place he had begun to think of as his very own. It was high noon. Jules had gone away to his dinner, and Hugh had, at least, half an hour to himself. He broke open the seals and began to read. Jeremy wrote good letters; he could make you see and feel and hear all that had gone on about him. And he had taken time to give to his young brother a full account of the voyage, of the heavy storms they had met on the way across, which broke spars and swept away rigging, and set everyone at work repairing the damage.

"I sailed as a clerk, but in the end I did something of everything on board ship, even to cooking the Captain's dinner when the cook had a damaged arm. I went aloft with the others, and am good enough, now, at clewing up and furling down. I like it; I would feel like signing on as a seaman for another voyage, except for the business we have in hand."

He—and Hugh also—had already seen England, but Denmark was something entirely new. "You should see how clean the whole country is, and how neat, everything in its place, and bright-colored and gay. I learned enough German in school to help me make something of the language; it will not be long before I can talk Danish and understand it. But, oh, it will be very long before we get our ships, Mr. Girard's and Grandfather's. Every person, every country, is still getting things in order after the wars of Napoleon's time. With Napoleon on one side and England on the other, each forbidding ships to come into European harbors with supplies, the vessels were seized right and left, and only a long, long untangling of laws will give them back, and the value of their cargoes.

"The Danes are fair, and if we can prove that they had no right to lay hands on vessels of a country that was not at war, we can get our own again. But the list of lawsuits is a tremendously long one—and who knows when the judges will get to ours? We have to stay here, one or the other of us, and keep reminding the men in charge that the business of furthering our affair must go on. When I have learned a little more, Mr. Greening will leave me here alone and will go back to England. Then he will come back and let me go away somewhere. But do not look for me at home again for a very long time."

The letter went on with messages to everyone, with advice to Hugh. Jeremy had not heard from home; he was anxious to know what they had managed to do. "I know how much you have wanted to help," he said. "I am wondering what you can find to do when you are twelve. I have found seventeen was not the oldest age in the world, and I could wish my years were more. But I will be eighteen and, maybe, more than that before this affair is done. But I am going to keep with it. I am bound that both Grandfather and Mr. Girard shall have what is justly due them."

Hugh put down the letter with a long sigh. How he wished that he were Jeremy, tall, old, carrying on real business, writing from across the sea about strange countries, about law courts and ships, a fight for justice! And he, what was he? A boy of twelve, a gardener's boy sitting here on the grass by the Delaware wishing and wishing he could do great things. But—the thought came flooding through him—after all, he was helping to hold things steady while Jeremy was away, while Grandfather's fortunes were so low. He could only do a little, but that little was, surprisingly, of very great help. Yes, he could do his part while Jeremy was doing his so far away. And—

why, what was he thinking of, he was forgetting Mr. Girard's letter!

It was very short, very formal and businesslike. "I have a report, by the ship just come in, of what your brother is doing, and how useful he is proving himself to be. It is not necessary for him to stay in Denmark continually. Therefore, since I have been asked to recommend, for a certain undertaking, a young man who is entirely to be trusted, I am thinking of suggesting your brother. I hope this step will have your approval. I trust that all goes well with your own enterprises."

There were many times in the next week or two that Hugh wondered whether all was really going well with his own undertaking. Jules was so friendly, but was such a hard worker himself that he had little mercy on anyone else. Hugh had thought that his employment would last through the summer perhaps, and then Jeremy would be at home again and all things would be different. But Jeremy had said, "I am seventeen; I will be eighteen before this affair is done." Once more Hugh wondered whether he could bear to wait? He was the sort of boy who said little about his impatience, but it surged within him nonetheless. He had almost given up his work once; the temptation to do so still came back again and again. It was surprising how a certain pricking curiosity about a dark-faced man peering through the bushes was still helping to hold him at his place. It helped him strangely, too, when he sat down for rest next to the oak tree, to feel its hard, firm trunk behind his shoulders. But this last he could not explain, except for the idea that the tree was his own.

In the middle of May Mr. Bonaparte went away for a little journey to see more of the sights of America than he knew so far. Mr. Mailliard was to go with him, for the expedition to Switzerland, if there was to be one, had not yet been arranged. Mr. Bodine was to go also, with five servants and three carriages, to make complete arrangements for Mr. Bonaparte's comfort on the way.

The day after they went, the mansion at Point Breeze was turned upside down and inside out in a furious tempest of house cleaning. The great velvet rugs had to be carried out upon the grass and beaten; the heavy hangings were taken down to be aired and brushed; the furniture was brought outside and the cushions cleaned. Even old Jules was drawn into the work of washing the great hall windows, with Hugh to help him. Madame Le Mar, who was in charge of the housekeeping in Mr. Bonaparte's mansion, was almost beside herself. It seemed that, since five servants had gone with Mr. Bonaparte and Mr. Mailliard, she felt she did not have enough left to carry out the business of setting the house in order. Hugh, working on the ladder just outside the window of the great salon, heard her lamenting.

"He will be gone less than a week," she kept saying. "We must finish before he returns. And they have taken Richard to clean their boots. It was always Richard's work to polish the brasses, and no one else will do it. What am I to do?" Her eye fell on Hugh. "You are a boy of this neighborhood. Find me someone whom I can bring in for the day to make the andirons and fire shovels shine as they should do."

Yes, Hugh could tell her of someone. "There is a girl

who lives in the same house I do; she is only a little younger than I, and she can work hard—she loves it. I see her scrubbing and polishing in the kitchen every morning. She will be glad to come."

"Then get her. Go this instant and fetch her. I am almost distracted with thinking about who is to do what."

Hugh almost ran the whole distance from Point Breeze to the Storrs' house. Hilda's school was having its spring holiday, so that he knew she would be there. He was so breathless that he could hardly explain his errand, but the important words tumbled out first. "Oh, Hilda, you are going to see the house."

It was probable that the two who worked the hardest through that long day of bustle and high activity at Point Breeze were the two youngest members of the whole busy company. Hugh and Hilda toiled straight on through all the confusion and tumult about them, through all the orders given and then changed or taken back. There were excited disputes: "This is not my work. You have no right, Madame, to ask me to set my hand to such a task!" "Ah, but Jacques, just on this day when we have so much to be done." "No, Madame, I followed our good master from France to serve his own person, but not to clean marble floors. No, Madame, that I cannot do."

Then would follow tears on the part of Madame Le Mar, a search for someone else whose dignity was not so high, the discovery that the next person did not know how to wash marble pavements and had no special desire to be told the most perfect manner in which it should be done— all this went forward while the spring winds blew through the great house, while the uncurtained windows let in the sun, and while hasty feet clattered and resounded on the bare floors. Hilda and Hugh, when they caught sight of each other, would exchange a grin of delight over the ridiculous scene about them. No one, it seemed, had any taste for washing windows, and old Jules firmly refused to climb a ladder. Therefore, the work fell upon Hugh. Inexperienced he certainly was, but he could run up and down the ladder like a monkey and did not mind how tall was the window he was called upon to clean.

Hilda was at last seeing every part of that large, splendid house she had so longed to enter. She was taking everything in, the beautiful pictures, the figures and the tapestries. Nothing, however, kept her from working diligently at every task set her. She progressed steadily from one room to another. She polished the fender and the great tall andirons in the fireplace of the grand salon, whose marble carvings, it was said, had come from Rome and been given as a present to Joseph Bonaparte by a Cardinal. She was taken next into the card room, then into the big dining room, then into the little "salon of the busts," where Joseph kept his relics of the great Emperor. The bronzes must be wiped off; the metal name plates on the pedestals must be made to shine again. Finally she was led upstairs by the excited and ever-talking Madame Le Mar to work in the library, on the second floor, which ran along the whole end of one wing nearest the Delaware River. Next to it were Mr. Bonaparte's bedroom and his dressing room. The fireplace of the library was huge, and the fire irons were big enough for giants; they must be rubbed and rubbed again. Hugh, on a high ladder, was polishing away at the tall panes of the windows that looked out on the river.

The bustle in the house was dying down; the carpets had been brought in and relaid; the curtains were folded and laid away to be put up again when the windows were finished. The bustling chattering company had drifted down to the servants' dining room to have tea, and only Hugh and Hilda, finally, were left at work upstairs.

Hilda had taken up her basket of clothes and cleaning powders and was about to move into the little dressing room next to Mr. Bonaparte's bedroom. She went to the door, then suddenly came running back, quick and frightened and making no noise. "Hugh," she whispered at the window, "come, come and see." He swung over the sill and followed her, both of them moving quietly. She partly opened the door, and together they peered through the crack.

There was a man standing in the next room, a thin man with a dark coat and, tied over it, a striped apron such as all the other French servants were wearing that day. He even had a brush in his hand, but he was not using it. He was moving rapidly and silently about, opening drawers and peeping into them, shutting them quickly and opening the next ones. He slipped the catch on the closet doors, looked in, closed them again with a frown of disappointment. He walked across to the door opposite, that which led into Mr. Bonaparte's bedroom. There stood the famous bureau of a hundred drawers. Was he going to search through that? He turned a little to open the inner door, and they could see him plainly.

Instantly Hugh knew who he was, knew again his thin, jutting nose, his narrow black eyebrows, his pale face. It was the man he had seen twice before on the hillside, who had run away to escape in his boat. He had, even now, a fine white shirt as before; the apron tied over it must be one which he had snatched up downstairs in the midst of the confusion. Any one of the other servants might have thought that he was merely an extra person brought in by Madame Le Mar for help with the unusual work. He might have been in the house for hours. Certainly nobody had questioned him, and little by little, he had worked his way upstairs until now, as his face plainly showed, he was at the place where he wished to be. He drew a little breath and grinned with satisfaction to himself as he opened the door. Then, in a flash, he caught sight of Hugh in the mirror opposite and turned.

The boy thought for an instant of calling for help, but help was too far away. He made one great stride, all across the little room, tried to seize the man's thin shoulder, and was instantly shaken off. He had a second of feeling that lean arm, thin and hard as steel, sweep back against him, cast him aside as though he were a fly. The man darted through Joseph's room and out by another door into the long library. He stumbled over the fire irons which Hilda had left standing against a table until the marble fireplace could be washed; he brought them down with a great clatter and must have bruised his shins sharply. He looked back at the two, his face drawn, his teeth showing; it was a look of anger, but of frantic terror also. The mischance had delayed him, and once more Hugh was upon him. The boy caught his sleeve, felt it slip through his fingers, and saw the man whip down the room and escape through the farther door. He was stronger, quicker, more determined than one could imagine any man could be. Panting now, Hugh still followed, Hilda left behind. Hugh ran through a hall and came out at the head of the great central staircase which the man had already begun to go down.

Like all stairs in grand houses, it was wasteful of distance; it separated at the top, extended in two directions, then turned and came together at the bottom. Hugh had seen once before those wide zigzags and had thought idly how a person would feel trying to run down them in a hurry. There was no chance that anyone so sure-footed would stumble, and the man was well ahead of him. Hugh swung himself over the banister, dropped, a long drop, to the floor below. The marble was hard, but he landed lightly. Yes, the move was a good one, for he was well ahead of the stranger now. Down the long corridor he heard the voices in the servants' dining room, the high chatter and laughing of people making no haste in the world over their tea. He shouted now, "Help, help!" Then, remembering himself, cried again in French, "Au secours, au secours!"

No one heard—the chattering was too high and loud, and drowned his voice. The man was upon him, seized him, swung him aside and flung him, sliding, all across the floor. The fellow was out by the garden door, across the lawn, escaping toward the bluff and the river. Hugh was still running but dropped far behind him now. The man did not seek the path; he took the short way, straight over the hill. A little creature jumped and dodged among the

bushes to get out of his way. It was the groundhog, taking
the sun peacefully before his house door in the pleasant
afternoon sun. And it was into that house door, into
the mouth of his hole, that the fleeing man stepped. He
stumbled, fell with a thud, and went rolling over and over
down the slope. He got up. It was plain that he was hurt,
that he could hardly stand. But his boat was only three
yards away. He dragged himself into it, pushed off with the
oars, and was out into the current of the river. As he swung
his boat to slide downstream, he looked back at Hugh and
raised his arm in a mocking gesture. He waved something
for a moment, and then flung it overboard. It was the
striped apron.

Hugh walked slowly up the slope. Hilda was standing at
the garden door. "I didn't call the rest," she said. "I thought
I would wait until you said what to do." They sat down on
the upper step and held counsel.

Once before Hugh had warned Mr. Bodine and had
been sharply rebuked. Would it do any good, now, to
take the matter to the excited and easily upset Madame
Le Mar? What could she do? Nothing. Hilda's father was
away from home; her mother and Hugh's mother were out
also. But Grandfather was there; he would know what to
advise; they would go back and ask him. They did not stop
to gather up their scattered properties but set off at once.
Madame Le Mar would have occasion to exclaim, when
she found their soap and polishing cloths, "Behold now
I know. There is no person to be trusted to work without
watching—no person in the world. And I had really had
some faith in these little Americans."

Grandfather was sitting in the sunny corner of the garden. Hugh's mother and Mrs. Storrs had gone to spend the afternoon and evening with a sick neighbor, so that he was alone. The robins were busy all about the grass, and two orioles were beginning a nest in the tree above him. He looked up at them without surprise.

"We want to talk to you about something," Hugh began. He told the whole thing, what he had thought when he saw the man before, how little use it was to speak to anybody in authority in the house. "If someone else reported it, someone like Mr. Girard, they would listen, I suppose," Hugh declared. "But Mr. Bodine does not think it proper to pay attention to a boy, and has made Mr. Bonaparte think so, too. And even now they and Mr. Mailliard are away."

Grandfather sat thinking for some minutes. "We should come back to what you said at the beginning. It is Mr. Girard who should know about this," he said finally. "And I think there is no better way than for you to go to Philadelphia and tell him yourself, at once. I believe that there should be no time lost."

"But how will I go?" Hugh said. "The stage passed at noon, and there will not be another from Bordentown to Philadelphia until day after tomorrow." So little travel was there on the Philadelphia road that the stage ran only every other day.

"But there is one from Burlington," Hilda suggested. "It leaves the Apple Tree Tavern at four o'clock in the morning. If you could get to Burlington tonight, somehow, and sleep at the tavern—my aunt lives there—do you remember we saw her at the market?—then you could start with the coach and get to Philadelphia soon after noon." It was always Hilda who seemed to know how matters should be arranged. Grandfather nodded approval. He put his hand into his pocket and pulled out, a little ruefully, a single dollar and a few pennies. Hugh searched his own; he, too, had a dollar, left from his last week's wages. The stage was two dollars; it hardly mattered that there would be only some pennies over. "How will you come back?" Hilda asked, and then answered the question herself. "There will be market on Saturday, and somebody will be coming home with a cart or a boat."

"And to get to Burlington?" Grandfather asked, for that, too, was a serious question. Old Dolly was away with Eleanor Armond and Betsy Storrs.

"I will have to walk to Burlington unless I can get a lift in a cart," Hugh said. But the prospect did not seem too hard. Hilda went in to make ready some supper for him before he set out.

He ate in haste, changed to a better jacket, put the two dollars into his pocket, and set out upon his way. Whatever strange matters were going on, with Point Breeze as their storm center, the outcome of them seemed to depend now upon himself—and Mr. Stephen Girard.

It was a warm May night. There is one kind of spring that comes in gardens, where people set out early flowering bulbs and plants, and are rewarded with bright blossoms almost before the robins come. There is another kind of spring which comes more slowly, more completely— the spring that spreads through the whole countryside,

touching the wild fruit trees in the woods first, so that their
clouds of thin small blossoms are visible from afar among
the bare trees, moving farther, spreading green grass and
opening leaves, bringing out the peach and cherry trees,
coming at last to its high tide, the moment when the apple
trees are in blossom.

He passed so many orchards that it seemed as though
the whole of New Jersey was one blowing garden of pink
and white. They were sending out clouds of sweetness, so
soft and delicate that one could hardly know the fragrance
was there, could only feel that the air was strangely blessed
that night with something beyond the ordinary. The sun
went down above the river; the twilight was so still that
the voices of the birds were very loud; the calling robins
were going across in a flock to roost in the woods opposite;
a single unseen red-winged blackbird sending out his
throaty whistle at regular intervals from down near the
shore.

Hugh had always been keenly alive to beautiful things;
he felt now that nothing he had ever known was quite
so beautiful as this spring night, so warm, fragrant, and
living all around him. It reminded him of music, the sort
of music he had heard in church with his mother one day
when his heart was more than usually open to the fullness
of all that was around him. "O, all ye works of the Lord,"
the choir had been singing, "sun and moon, showers and
dew, light and darkness, bless ye the Lord." That, it seemed
to him, was how it was tonight. "O, all ye green things
upon the earth, bless ye the Lord." As he walked on there
seemed to drop away from him the doubts and despairs

and hesitations which had gone with his work and his waiting; he knew that he would have strength to go on. He knew that, after all, it was not true that everything depended on him, that all that was needed from him was that he do his best, his very best, and that somehow everything would come together for good in the end, even the long waiting for his brother.

The moon came up, clear and white, so that the orchards turned to the whiteness of frost, a still whiteness that hung upon the trees as though a breath of wind would blow it all away. Hugh listened with every step for the creak of a cart wheel or the sound of horses' hoofs, but no person was abroad on the river road that night. The moon rose high and made the road a flowing highway of white before him; his black shadow marched beside—it was his only company.

Hugh had ten miles to cover; that was a good way to go. The road followed, in and out, the winding of the Delaware. It would have been better if he could have gone as the crows flew, flapping home to their roost across the treetops and above the white fields. Hugh knew all the landmarks: this sharp turn was three miles from Bordentown; this dip into a hollow with a little brook gurgling under a stone bridge told him that he had now walked five. He began to feel tired, to feel sleepy so that he staggered once or twice, blind with drowsiness. Then his wits seemed to wake again, and to bend themselves to one thing, to drive him onward. He seemed to have turned into a machine that walked and walked and walked and had no feeling and no thought of any kind. He was almost surprised, almost daunted when he found that he was passing between houses, when he caught sight of the warm yellow lights of the windows of the tavern and heard the faint creaking of its sign swinging above the door.

CHAPTER 5

The Philadelphia Coach

Travelers were likely to stop late at the door of the Apple Tree Tavern, so that Jenny Topham, Hilda's plump and rosy aunt, showed no surprise when there was a knock at the door and a very weary wayfarer came in. She did raise her eyebrows a little when she noted the age of her new guest.

But she only asked, "How can I serve you, sir? A bite of hot supper? I could get it ready in a moment."

Her respectfulness made Hugh feel ten times more a man and, as a result, ten times less weary. He answered that he thought he would have a—a— He hesitated over the thought of what to ask for, since hot food would have made him over into a new being, but he remembered the extra coppers jingling in his pocket and knew that they could buy him very little.

But his voice seemed to recall to him Mrs. Topham's memory, for now she exclaimed, "There now, aren't you Hugh Armond who is living with my sister Betsy Storrs? Of course you are, and anything in the house we have you are welcome to. You're to sleep here and take the coach in the morning, did you say? Bless me, don't tell me that you walked all the way from Bordentown. Just come out to the kitchen, will you? My husband and helpers are all out, and I'm alone in the tavern. If you will pardon it, I can serve you a better and hotter meal in there by the fire."

Hugh was quite willing. After that long, lonely journey he was glad, indeed, of the company of good Mrs. Topham in the kitchen. He helped to stir up the fire and to bring more wood, while she set pots to boiling and put a pudding to warm in the brick oven. It was a fine meal that he ate by the fire, toasting his shins, for the night had grown cool, and the warmth of the fire was most welcome. He had just finished and leaned back in his chair when the door in the main room was heard to open and another guest came in. The sound of his feet was slow and heavy and uneven, as though he were lame or limping. Mrs. Topham went in to see what he wanted.

Hugh heard a man's voice speaking clear and rather thin, a voice with a foreign sound. The guest gave his orders abruptly. He wanted a fire built and supper brought in; he gave elaborate directions as to what he would like, and directed that a room be made ready upstairs at once.

"You do not keep a good inn if you do not have a good fire ready and burning when guests come," he said at the end.

Mrs. Topham did not take his rebuke with any humility. "We do not usually expect guests to be out on the road so late as this," she returned. "Yes, I will get your supper ready and your room, but you will have to wait a few minutes." She walked out with her head high, while the man sat down at one of the tables.

"I don't know what to make of him," she said to Hugh in a whisper in the kitchen. "He has been here before. He gives the name of Mr. Dominic, and he always behaves the same. Orders one about—do this, do that—as though he were some great gentleman, but I vow he did not even have a horse to ride up to our door. He is limping, too. Now how could he have come here walking and so lame as that?" She kept asking herself questions to which there were no answers, as she bustled about, prepared another supper and went in to lay the table. She hurried back and forth, serving his meal, looking hot and flushed and angry as she came out with the empty dishes. After she had cleared the table, and was just turning to go upstairs to make his room ready, there was an impatient rapping on the table. His voice, harsh and thin, came through the door. "I told you to bring more ale. What sort of service is this?" Mrs. Topham was near to weeping with nervousness and vexation.

Hugh got up from his place by the fire. "I will take it in to him," he offered, picking up the jug from the table. "Do not stop. Go up and get his room ready, and I will get whatever he wants."

He went into the next room, saw the traveler sitting at the table, and for an instant stopped, transfixed, on the threshold. The man's dark, narrow face, his thin cheekbones, low black eyebrows— Hugh had seen them all before. This fellow who called himself Dominic was the one whom Hugh had seen last darting out of Mr. Bonaparte's room, whipping down the long staircase, flinging himself through the door to escape by the river.

This was the very man. And in that sudden moment he knew also that the fellow was very young, not really much older than Jeremy, young and worn out and disheartened. Hugh's first feeling had been a wave of alarm at recognizing him; in another breath he felt all terror drop away and knew only that this was someone who must be bested somehow, by some means, but who was no longer mysterious and terrible.

No one could have noticed that fraction of a second that Hugh stopped at the door before he came in. It was possible that, in another jacket, and with his hair brushed smooth, he might look so different that the fellow would not know him again. So it seemed, for Mr. Dominic scarcely looked up, merely grumbled as the ale was poured into his glass. Mrs. Topham came down presently to say that the room was ready and the fire lighted upstairs. She breathed a sigh of relief, and Hugh did also, when the fellow went upstairs at last. Silas Topham came home soon after, and Hugh mounted to the little room in the peak of the house to sleep for a few hours until he should be woken to catch the coach.

He woke to hear voices in the innyard below and knew that he had little time if he were to catch the coach. He tumbled into his clothes, swallowed a hasty breakfast, thanked Mr. Topham as best he could, and went out to take his place. A certain uneasy misgiving had been in his mind all night, even through his dreams. The coachman climbed to his box, the horses pawed and plunged to be off, the last package was put in place; they were ready to go. But no, it could not be, what Hugh had thought was, after all, bound to come out. The inn door flew open, Mr. Dominic came hurrying out, still limping, and climbed to a place on the top of the coach. And now they were really off. The man was sitting near to Hugh, in the next seat but one, yet he seemed to take no notice of the boy's being near him.

There had been rain in the night, and now the wind was coming up so that the apple blossoms were falling and the breeze was throwing the petals in white handfuls all about the grass. The fields looked dark with their wet furrows, with the rows of springing corn and the smooth green carpet of wheat spread out on each side of the road. Everyone on the coach was sleepy and silent, so that there was little sound but the light spinning of the wheels and the steady thud of the horses' hoofs. They stopped now and again to pick up passengers at this crossroad or that.

A shy little woman climbed up, bearing a basket of live ducks, and, since the coach was getting crowded, had much trouble to squeeze in next to Mr. Dominic. He moved impatiently and exclaimed aloud to the man beyond him: "I thought this was a coach and not a farmyard. What will they take on next?"

The poor little woman turned very pink, and the man addressed spoke up in her defense. "You do not understand the state of New Jersey, sir, nor the traffic on its roads. The state is, you observe, a wide plain between two rivers, two very noble rivers, sir. The great explorer, Henry Hudson himself, found and named them the North River and the South River, although we have now come to call the North River the Hudson and the South River the Delaware."

Dominic tried to interrupt, but the flow of information went steadily on. "Each river makes a great seaport, and so a great city. It is the task of the State of New Jersey, sir, it is bound to be her occupation, to supply food for these two cities. Those who live softly and comfortably in the houses and taverns of New York or Philadelphia may be glad, indeed for the peaches and apples, the fat geese and fresh eggs that New Jersey brings to the cities' doors. But you could not be expected to understand these things, sir, being so plainly a foreigner. And not from France, either, I take it, though we have many Frenchmen among us now, with all the troubles that have been going on across the sea."

Mr. Dominic gave some growl of a reply, but since every person on the coach turned a head to stare at him when the word foreigner was spoken, he said nothing further to bring attention on himself or to draw further conversation from his neighbor. The way seemed long and more and more ducks and hens were taken on until the coach was laden more with poultry than passengers. They rattled through Camden at last, crossed the river on the ferry, and were clattering over the cobblestones of the streets of Philadelphia. And now, for the first time, Hugh's fellow passenger turned about and spoke to him.

"It seems that we both keep on journeying in the same direction. Will I have the pleasure of having my ale poured out by you again, when I take supper tonight at the Black Eagle Tavern on Dock Street?"

Hugh was so taken aback that he found no words to answer. The coach stopped a moment after and, seeing suddenly that he was near to Water Street, he climbed down without a word. The other had his head over his shoulder and was looking back at him intently as the coach turned the corner and disappeared into Market Street.

At the office in Water Street there was a line of people waiting to see Mr. Girard, but a clerk motioned to Hugh, led him through a side door, so that he should not seem to be taken in before the others, and brought him through a short passage into Mr. Girard's room. His friend looked tired, and the table was piled with papers. But he sat, listening intently, as Hugh, without wasting time or words, told his story. Mr. Girard did not interrupt, but nodded quietly when he was finished.

"A man, you say, almost as young as your brother, and speaking with an accent that is not American nor yet French?" He thought for more than a minute and then nodded his head. "Yes, I have thought and wondered about certain things and have come to my own conclusion. I will tell you what it is that the man desires, what Mr. Bonaparte rather unwisely keeps in his house."

He pushed the papers away and leaned back in his chair. Hugh settled himself to listen. "You must know that this Joseph Bonaparte used often to act as secretary to his brother, the Emperor Napoleon, receiving and writing letters for him. For a time Napoleon was the most powerful man in Europe. Kings and princes, Czar of Russia and Emperor of Austria were all afraid of him. They wrote him letters in which they flattered his greatness, they begged for favors, they even begged for mercy. Those letters our friend Joseph, so he once told me, still has in his possession.

There are many in high places who would be glad to have them back, lest they ever be given to the public, lest their begging and their flattery should be known. One attempt after another has been made to demand them, to buy them even, but Joseph has refused. Now someone is bound to have them by any means possible, and has hired this youth for the undertaking. Have you any idea from his speech what country he is from?"

"I am not sure," Hugh said. "I once heard a Russian at my father's house who talked something like him."

"He might be Russian or Polish," Girard agreed. "He may also be a man of no great evil in himself, but who has been forced into this by those who have power to make him do it. I am even a little sorry for him. But, just the same, his activities must stop, for he may do much harm before he is done. Mr. Bonaparte has thought that here in America he would be safe from all the stresses and dangers that rise out of a time when men seize power and other men try to take it from them. But when the world has been in such turmoil as Napoleon Bonaparte has brought about, one cannot be sure of untroubled peace and security anywhere, even so far away as this."

"We could find the man," Hugh suggested, "for he said plainly he was going to the Black Eagle Tavern on Dock Street."

"There is no Black Eagle Tavern on Dock Street," Mr. Girard told him, "nor do I remember having heard the name of any such inn anywhere in Philadelphia. I will send someone to all the taverns to inquire for a man of his description."

The clerk came to announce that the Building Committee of the new hospital had come to see Mr. Girard. Hugh got up, for he knew he should go. "I must talk to these men who have arranged a meeting with me," his friend said, "but tonight I expect to set out on a little journey to look at some property in Bucks County. If you will go with me, we can come back by way of Bordertown, and I can inquire further into this matter of Mr. Bonaparte's, which, in truth, gives me much concern."

Yes, Hugh would like greatly to go with him. "Then," declared Stephen Girard, "we must use a little strategy so that we two may slip out of the city of Philadelphia without being drawn into any matters which will hold us. Do you know that large house on Fifth Street that is close to where your good Betsy Storrs has her market stall? The lower part of it is made into shops, but if you climb the stair to the second floor and knock at the first door, a little old woman, Madame Estelle Duane, will let you in, and there wait for me until I come. I will find some way to get away as soon as I can."

Hugh was let out by a side door and made his way through the streets, quiet and empty in the stillness of the spring evening. He knew the house well toward which he was walking; he had often looked up at it, tall and stately beyond the row of market stalls that stretched down the middle of the street. It was simple and square and solid, but very shabby now. The lamps before it and the stone facing around the windows made him think it must have been a great house in its day. He climbed the stair as he had been told, knocked, and was admitted at once by the brisk little woman with a white cap and wavy white hair.

"Mr. Girard sent you?" she said in answer to Hugh's message. "Then you are a very favored friend of his, for he does not direct many people here. You look tired, lad, and sleepless, as though you had traveled far. If you are to wait long, you might snatch an hour of rest before Monsieur Etienne comes." It was so that she always spoke of him, for as a very young girl she had been a servant in his father's house in Bordeaux, and could not use any other name than his French one. She had come to America some years after he had, and had worked for him so faithfully that he had provided for her old age. She lived alone in this little apartment, where she was always busy and need never feel want.

"I was with him when he was first married, when he still lived in the little house in Mount Holly. What misfortune that his beautiful wife is now such an invalid. I have been so proud to see him rise to such power and importance."

She was laying out supper for Hugh as she talked, speaking in French, and with delight at his understanding her tongue. She set the table beside the big window with its broad sill. Hugh looked about him at the square room with its white woodwork, its high ceiling, and carving about the fireplace, all rather plain, but certainly of great dignity. "It is a very fine room," he said, when her chatter paused for a minute.

"Ah, did you not know what house this is? It is the mansion in which Mr. George Washington lived while he resided in Philadelphia as President of the United States. They have changed it much there below, where the shops were made, but here above you can still see what sort of a house was chosen for America's first president."

Hugh saw the other rooms and liked their cool white plainness. As he sat by the window he could look down Market Street, so broad was it, to see the blue Delaware running at its foot. Here President Washington himself might have sat, he thought, and looked at the river flowing past. He must have missed his great blue Potomac, for he was not used to living in cities, people said, and that glimpse of moving water must often have been a comfort to him. Hugh had talked often with his grandfather about President Washington.

An hour later Mr. Girard came in, looking more weary than ever but smiling with relief that the labors of the day and the week were over, and now he could be free. He reported that the man he had sent to inquire at the taverns had found no trace of any such person as Dominic. "He meant to deceive you," he said to Hugh. "He must have some friend who shelters him."

It was growing dark as they went through the streets; the street lights were coming out, orange in the dusk as the lamplighter went from one to another, set his ladder against the post, and climbed up to light the lamp in the lantern at the top.

"I sent you word through François Bodine," Mr. Girard was telling Hugh. "I wanted you to know what we have arranged for Mr. Mailliard's journey into Switzerland. I did not tell you before, lest it could not be managed. But, as I told you in a letter, we needed a young man, and one completely to be trusted. And so I sent word to your brother Jeremy to meet him in Geneva. I know that he is not needed continuously in Copenhagen, and Mailliard could have no better companion."

"Oh," cried Hugh, "oh! And Mr. Bodine never told me." Bitterness welled up within him, for he might have known of the plan weeks ago. It made Jeremy nearer, somehow, to know of some special thing he was doing.

They went on until it was long after dark. Hugh was so drowsy when they finally stopped at an inn to spend the night that he could never have told what place of hospitality it was. He stumbled upstairs and slept, undreaming, until it was day.

If Mr. Stephen Girard had looked worn and tired the day before in his crowded office in the city, he was a new man when he rolled forward through the country, with the weariness disappearing from his face and his spirits rising visibly. He owned farms, here and there, so he told Hugh, but he was always open to the pleasant thought of buying another.

"Whenever my captains go to far countries, I tell them to bring me back plants and seeds which might grow in this climate. I have some grapevines whose like is not to be found in America, I do believe, and I train and prune all my fruit trees myself. You see, I like to boast a little, as one man who likes to grow things boasts to another. I believe Mr. Bonaparte has got himself a good assistant gardener for Point Breeze."

Hugh's cheeks burned. "I—I am not so sure of that," he said. "Once—once, I thought old Jules was so hard on me that I was going to leave everything and go away. But I have learned to understand Jules now, and he has taught me much and has given us many things for Storrs' garden. We are going to have anemones in the autumn, something like the Roman ones they sell on the street in Paris. Do you remember?"

"Oh, I was a lad of the provinces," Stephen Girard said. "Only once or twice in my life did I go up to the great city of Paris; but when I did, I dwelt on its wonders for months afterward. I am a Republican, Monsieur Hugh, and I have not thought well of all those things which have gone on in France since Napoleon rose to power. So I returned but once to my native country, and find that I do not wish to do so again."

"And yet you have helped Mr. Joseph Bonaparte," Hugh said.

"Oh, yes," agreed Girard. "I will gladly help any man who is in adversity; and even though Joseph lives in what is almost a palace and has, it seems, all the money he needs to spend, yet he is nonetheless in adversity, for he is forbidden to return to his own land."

They stopped before noon to look at the farm, a fine rolling stretch of acres on flat, high ground some miles west of the Delaware. Mr. Girard went over it carefully, looking at the trees and the pigs, the cows and the pigeons. But at last he shook his head.

"I think I will not buy it," he said to the owner. "The slope of the land is not what I want, and it will not grow the fruit and vines that I like best. But I will see what I can do to find you a purchaser. It is good land." They got into the carriage again and journeyed on, their faces set now toward the Delaware and toward Bordentown on the other side.

It was almost evening when they came near to where they were to cross the river. Mr. Girard spoke to his coachman, and the horses turned aside down a grass-grown lane. "There is a good place that I would like to show you," he said. "And there is time." They passed a farmhouse and a green meadow and at last drew up close to the river on a stretch of open ground where bushes and trees and a broken wall showed that here had once been a great house and a garden going down to the water.

"Here," Stephen Girard said, "was once set the dwelling of Mr. William Penn, who planted this colony of Pennsylvania and decreed that all who lived in it should be free and unquestioned as to what they thought or what they believed. Other colonies, in the end, followed his good example and his good ideas, and so America has become a safe, free country to which many a man has fled when the old lands were too hard for him to bear. It was the place for me to come to live, for above all, I dislike quarrels between creeds and churches. It was a great house Mr. Penn had here, plain, as are Quaker houses, beautiful in its plainness and its dignity. I remember it, for it was still standing when I came to America. It is good to think that he was very happy here. You have seen the houses of two great men, Monsieur Hugh, Washington's and Penn's. They match but strangely the house of that man who dwells across the river, who lives, we may say, by the borrowed greatness of his brother. Joseph Bonaparte has done all he could to set up here, in America, such a house as stands for Napoleon and his fame and greatness. He hopes, I feel sure, that his brother will someday come to dwell in it."

Hugh stared at him, and said in startled surprise, "He expects—that?" but Girard was going on and did not heed.

"You saw what simplicity was good enough for Washington. You see how little of lasting glory William Penn put into his house. Glory—that was a thing of which neither of those two men thought. When there was a revolution in our country, Washington fought for liberty and won it. Then he set himself, with the same hope and energy, to build up a nation and to make sure that liberty, once won, should be kept forever. And in France, there was a revolution there also—Napoleon was leader of the armies which fought for it. And when that liberty was won—what then? Napoleon took the power into his own hands. And so he ruled and fought and seemed to win glory for France, until all the world was against her. And in the end he fell through his own overreaching. It is only when I think of a man like Napoleon that I understand how great a man was Washington."

The breeze from the river was stealing up over the banks. A big black-trunked cherry tree was dropping the last of its petals as the wind shook its branches. It was a tree that William Penn had planted, Stephen Girard said, for Mr. Penn, too, had loved to make things grow in this soft, pleasant climate of Delaware.

The arrival at Point Breeze was not until well after dark. Hugh was told to get down from the carriage first and ask whether Mr. Bonaparte had come back. Madame Le Mar met him in the hall and greeted him coldly. Yes, it was

true that Hilda had come to explain that Hugh had gone
to Philadelphia on important business. But what business,
pray, could be more important than to finish the window
washing in time for Mr. Bonaparte's return? Hugh was
to come next morning as early as possible to work on
the windows again. But when she saw the distinguished
guest coming in behind him, she forgot Hugh entirely. Mr.
Girard must certainly stay all night that he might see His
Excellency in the morning, for, so she explained, the party
was returning before noon. And when Mr. Girard shook
hands with Hugh to bid him goodnight, when he said he
was coming to his house to see his grandfather tomorrow
and bade his coachman take Hugh home, then her eyes
were wide with wonder indeed.

The next day, after Mr. Bonaparte had returned, after he
and Mr. Girard had held a long consultation in the library,
Hugh saw his friend once more as he was about to take
leave. Mr. Bonaparte had come to the door with him, and
the two seemed to be arguing to the very end.

"I assure you I will be more watchful, my dear friend,"
Joseph Bonaparte was saying. "It is not possible for me to
give up what I am keeping here; it is a reminder of my old
life and of my brother's glories, with which I do not like
to part. But we will watch; we will watch with the greatest
vigilance."

Things settled down to be very quiet at Point Breeze.
The weeks went by, and it was full summer. The garden was
in its glory and did great credit to old Jules and to Hugh.
In August, Mr. Mailliard, with a great equipment of boxes
and trunks and bags and letter cases, set off on a journey.

No one had been told exactly whither he was bound, and there were only a few in the household who really knew his errand. How François Bodine made a great show of knowing, and of being forbidden to talk of the matter! How the others would have stared had they known that Hugh knew also! But Mr. Mailliard said goodbye to him and gave him a kind smile. "I understand that I am to have your brother as a traveling companion," he said. Hugh could hardly speak as he drove away. What would he not have given to be going also!

The days of summer were hot and lagged heavily. There was a good deal of work to do in weeding and watering, but it was not so interesting as the laying out and planting had been. Sometimes he almost wished that the threatening Dominic would show his face again, just to break the dullness of the passing days. But his last visit seemed to have given the foreign youth cause for alarm, since weeks and months went by and, though Hugh watched all the time, he never caught sight of him.

Little by little his hopes began to center on one thing, a thing not so very possible but still one that might come to pass. What if Jeremy should come home with Mr. Mailliard! He had letters from his brother; he was just starting from Denmark to join Mr. Mailliard. Then Mr. Bonaparte had letters. Mr. Mailliard had been wrecked on the coast of Ireland, but had saved all his possessions and was going forward with his journey. Finally the news came that Mailliard and Jeremy had met and were setting out for Switzerland. Once Mailliard's errand was finished, he would come directly home. Oh, surely, surely, Jeremy would come with him!

It was autumn and the flowers had lost their glory, the trees above the river were changing color, and Hugh's oak tree had put on a burnished scarlet that was like flame. Hugh could work only part of every day, for he had to go to school. He liked the simplicity and quiet of the school in the little brick building. In some ways, he knew more than the others. In some ways, a good deal less. He could have got his lessons easily, but, in fact, only half his attention was on them; with the other half he was always thinking of Jeremy. In the hours after school he still worked at Point Breeze. Mr. Bonaparte paid him almost as much now, for this part of the day, as Hugh had earned in the beginning. Madame Le Mar and others turned to him, to ask him to do things that were not easy. He was still the gardener's boy, but he was also a settled member of that big household, a person to be liked and trusted. Mr. Bonaparte always bade him good morning when he passed. Hugh felt that, in some odd, unspoken way, these two, he and the man who had once been a king, were growing to be friends.

Then it was late autumn. Hugh and Jules were putting the garden to bed for the winter. The oak kept its brown leaves but the other trees were bare. The days were often raw, and Hugh would have to run in and warm his hands at the fire inside. He had worked so late one afternoon that Madame Le Mar asked him to stay for supper. The butler had rheumatism in his hands, and she wondered whether Hugh would help in polishing some silver that must be ready, since guests were coming tomorrow. One of the grooms would take him home when he had finished.

Hugh worked hard, but there was more to do than anyone had thought, and it is possible that the work did not go quite so quickly as it might, for Gaston the butler, who had served Joseph Bonaparte in Spain, sat by, and, in return for the help Hugh was giving him, entertained him with all the tales that he knew, gay tales which kept them both in peals of laughter. Thus it was late when Hugh finished, put on his coat, and went out toward the stables to look for the man who was to take him home.

It was very dark, and a thin sprinkling of snow had begun to fall. Hugh stood still on the grass; he thought he heard the sound of horses' feet. There were many guests at Point Breeze, but few of them arrived as late as this. But it was quite true that a carriage was coming quickly up the drive; it drew up at the door, and Hugh came forward to see if anything was wanted. A man got out, wrapped in a traveling cloak, the snow powdering down upon him. The coachman was taking down boxes and bags. "Here, carry these in," the traveler said to Hugh. It was Mr. Mailliard.

Hugh loaded himself with all that he could carry and followed the secretary into the house. Without stopping, Mr. Mailliard went straight upstairs, and Hugh, not knowing what else to do, went after him. A sleepy servant looked out of a corridor and cried in astonishment, "You would speak to Mr. Bonaparte now? You would wake him from his sleep?"

"Yes," Mailliard answered. "That is what I am going to do."

He knocked loudly at Mr. Bonaparte's door. A drowsy

and surprised voice answered, finally. Mailliard pushed
the door open and went in. Hugh could see only a corner
of the room, but he heard the voices plainly. "Mailliard, I
thought it might be you. I am delighted to see you. And
what—what have you brought?"

Mailliard laughed, an odd excited laugh. He pulled out a
table from the wall, drew a package from his belt, opened a
case and poured out upon the table such a stream of jewels
as might have graced the most impossible fairy tale. Hugh
saw emeralds winking green in the candlelight, the sharp
whiteness of diamonds, the glow of rubies. "They are all
there," Mailliard said. "Just as we buried them, we two, that
night before you went to meet your brother."

Hugh turned about. He was not meant to watch and
listen, but he stood guard outside the door, for this was no
scene upon which any chance person should break in. The
door was closed finally, but he stood waiting. He had heard
Joseph asking excited questions; he had one to ask of his
own. He waited a very long time until finally Mr. Mailliard
came out. He looked pleased and elated, highly wrought
up by the success of his journey. "Why," he said to Hugh, "I
did not mean that you should wait. But no one else seems
to be awake. Will you carry my bags into my apartment?"

Hugh did as he was bid and, as he set down the last,
put his great question. "My brother, what of him, Mr.
Mailliard? Did—did he come back with you?"

For a moment Mr. Mailliard looked blank. "Your
brother? Oh, it was Jeremy. A good companion he made,
and most greatly to be trusted. Mr. Girard chose well in
sending him to meet me. I had forgotten that he was your

brother."

"But did he come back with you?" Hugh insisted desperately.

"No, no, he did not come back. He still had work to do on the other side. That task in Denmark will not be done, I fear, for a long time still. Thank you, my young friend, and goodnight." He closed the door. Hugh was left to walk along the passage, down the vast empty staircase, and through the marble-paved hall, all alone, his heart feeling dry and empty, disappointment wrapping him around like a cloak. Must he go on, could he go on, with Jeremy to be so long away?

CHAPTER 6

Dominic

If it had not been for Hilda! . . . Hugh thought of that
a great many times as the weeks went by. His mother
understood how hard the days had come to be for him—
they were hard for her too; Hugh was not blind to that.
But weeks and months do not mean quite so much to
someone who has seen more of them than has a boy of
twelve. Eleanor Armond had seemed to change ever since
she came to live in America again, even Hugh could see
it. She was calmer, more cheerful, and her face began
to take on a look of peace and untroubled contentment
which was new to her son. She worked in the garden and
her face was tanned and rosy; she helped Mrs. Storrs and
went with her on various errands about the neighborhood,
to see sick babies, to help a friend here and there when
there was a need, for Eleanor Armond made friends with
everyone and everyone loved her. She took the most wise
and beautiful care of Grandfather, so that he was far more
comfortable and happy in the upper room of the Storrs'
cottage than he had been in his great house.

But, just because Hugh knew how much his mother was
hungering in her own heart for the return of Jeremy, he

could not say too much to her about it. When they worked
on the flower borders or made ready the cold frames for
the new winter, they talked of other things, of the best of
their days in France, of the odd and interesting places in
Philadelphia, of the things that Eleanor Armond had done
and seen when she was a little girl in America—which
Hugh was to do and see in his own good time. Once they
took the chaise and old Dolly and drove the thirty miles
to Princeton, where Hugh saw the gray stone buildings,
the broad trees, and the wide sunny lawns of the college.
It all had such an air of wise quiet, of the long-gathered,
sunny, happy peace of the thousands of gay spirits who
had worked and learned there, that Hugh felt it was a place
unlike anything that he had ever known.

"This is where you are going to study in a few years," his
mother said, and Hugh was well content that it should be
so.

But the first step toward college was the attending, as
well as possible, to what he was learning in the little school
at Bordentown. Hugh had found it hard to apply his mind
to arithmetic and Latin when he was thinking of such
very different things—of his work in the garden, of old
Jules' chatter, of his mother working so hard—and always
coming back again and again to a picture of the waterfront
in Philadelphia—of the docks, of the ships coming in
from France one after another, of the one, the one which
would surely come in time, that would bring his brother
home. His mind wandered so much that Mrs. Cameron,
the teacher, a kindly plump lady with graying hair, used
to have to remind him now and again, "Hugh, come back

from wherever you have gone." He brought his mind back dutifully and bent himself to the lesson before him. But he would not have done well, he would indeed have not gone forward at all, if it had not been for Hilda.

They had been going to school for two months before she said anything, for Hilda was a person who waited until she was certain what she wanted to say before she spoke. She took the matter up with him as they walked home from school one afternoon in late October. Usually Hugh went home with the boys and Hilda with the girls, as was the custom, but today he had waited late because Mrs. Cameron had said he must have a perfect Latin lesson before he could go. It was not at all hard to get it perfect once he set his mind to it, and he was soon finished. When he came out, he found that Hilda had not yet gone. Mrs. Cameron was walking along behind them as they went home down the lane together, and ordinarily Hilda would have waited to walk beside her. But today she had something to say to Hugh.

"We were all so sure you were going to be the very head of the school," she said, beginning quite abruptly. "When you came, everyone was excited—you had seen so much; you had been to so many places. We thought we were going to be able to tell other people that we had a boy in our school, who had lived in France, who had traveled in Spain—tell them how much he knew."

Hugh was completely taken aback. "Why, what do you mean?" he asked. And then, as surprise began to turn into something else, he added a little angrily, "Why do you care?"

"We all care," Hilda answered with spirit. "We want to be proud of having you here. Even Mrs. Cameron, she would like to say to other teachers, 'I have a boy in my school who has seen Napoleon.' And they will say, 'How wonderful,' and 'What is he like? The boy, I mean, not Napoleon.' And she will have to tell them that he doesn't get his history lessons and stays in after school to do his Latin."

Hugh walked on for some minutes without saying anything. The lane was dusty and the day had been long, and altogether he felt in a very bad mood to be rebuked, especially by Hilda, who was a year younger than he. Also, Hugh was one of those boys to whom it never occurs that people would think or talk about him. He was nobody in particular, in his own eyes; he was just Hugh. What did Hilda mean by saying such strange things?

But Hilda seemed to know very well what she meant, for, at that minute did she seem to care very much what he thought of her. Her cheeks were very pink, and she looked down, as she always did when she was troubled, but she went straight on with what she had to say.

"It makes your mother anxious. Did you know that it did? She has said things to you sometimes about it, but you haven't even known that she was trying to make you see that you ought to do better."

Hilda could have said something else, she could have added, "And what will your brother think when he comes back and finds how little you have learned?" Hugh winced, thinking this was to come next. But Hilda did not say it. She had another shot to fire and she did. It came very surprisingly. "What is more, if you don't begin soon to do better, I am going to beat you. I am almost up with you now."

Hugh turned his head and stared at her. Could this really be the shy, quiet Hilda whom he thought he knew so well? It seemed that when Hilda had really made up her mind about anything, she had courage to say what she thought. And what she threatened was, in a way, possible. He was in her class in arithmetic because he had studied a different kind in France. Though he was far quicker at his sums, he was careless also, and Hilda, if she bent herself to it, might very easily outdo him and go on to a higher class. And in history she was behind him; but if she really wanted to, she could catch up there. It was most astonishing. "You wouldn't do that!" he exclaimed.

"I wouldn't want to," Hilda admitted. "I would have to work dreadfully hard. But I could, and if I thought it would make you do better, I would." They were passing a gate in a hedge and she stopped. "My mother wanted me to tell Mrs. Higgins something," she said and darted in. Not even she could have talked about this matter any further.

Hugh walked home, wondering, too much surprised to be really angry even. Finally he threw back his head and laughed. And he had thought that he knew Hilda so well! But it was from that day that things began to change in school. He began to think, even though it was the one thing Hilda had not put into words, "I can talk to Jeremy about this thing I am learning now, when he comes home." And sometimes, when his mind was wandering from his work, the sight of Hilda's brown head bent over her book brought him back to himself with a jerk. It was not so much what she had threatened to do that had awakened him. It was the idea of how hard she would be willing to work to make him do his best. For Hilda did not really like very much to study so hard from books. She liked animals and birds and flowers and fields full of sunshine and wind, just as he did.

There was someone else with whom he began to be really acquainted, after thinking all along that he knew him and what he was like. This was Mr. Bonaparte. Living in America had begun to change him, too, just as it had altered Hugh and his mother. People round about were coming more and more to visit Mr. Bonaparte. Monsieur and Madame Le Mar presided over his entertainments; for Madame Bonaparte, his wife, who had once been Queen Julie of Spain, was kept by ill health from crossing the Atlantic. She lived in Italy, for no one of the name of Bonaparte could come into France. Nobody ever spoke of Joseph now as the King of Spain. He used another title to which he had a right; he was called the Count of Survilliers. He had taken the name from one of the villages of his estate in France. Hugh knew how much he loved that place, how often his mind went back to it. Jules used to tell him of it, of the broad avenues and winding drives and tall, well-kept woods. "He desires to make this place like it," Jules said. "He is getting more and more interested in building up something that will stand for everything he loved there."

Jules liked to speak of him as Monsieur le Comte; but he did not seem to mind that Hugh talked of him as Mr.

Bonaparte and he used the name sometimes also, as good Republicans did in France. Joseph would get up early and come out in the plainest kind of clothes, carrying a hatchet with which, as he walked here and there over the grounds, he would mark trees that were to be cut, and lop off the ends of branches which were growing too large and in the way. There were more and more little groves of shrubs and small trees, more and more steps and statues, bridges and summerhouses. Every ship that came in seemed to bring something for Point Breeze, a picture, a roll of damask for curtains, a box containing a marble bust or a bundle of shrubs and a package of seeds. The big house began to seem crowded, but the grounds were still too large to be filled up so quickly. The garden behind the house had been a blaze of glory all summer. It was to be extended now and new beds and walks and hedges were being planned.

Mr. Bonaparte had actually begun to take notice of Hugh as part of his regular establishment, even to talk to him, to discuss with him some of his plans and intentions. As the weather grew cold with autumn, Jules was more and more laid by with rheumatism and Hugh had much of the work among the flowers to do alone. After the first snow came down, there was little further to be done, however, but Hugh had orders to come every Saturday to Point Breeze to do errands and finish small pieces of work that some of the others would not do. On one snowy morning in December he was told that Mr. Bonaparte wanted him, and he found his employer in the front hall, wrapped up to the eyes in a great fur lined overcoat and with a wool cap drawn down over his ears. In his hand was the faithful hatchet.

"We are going on a little expedition," Mr. Bonaparte said. "I wish to do something which I have always done myself on every place that I have owned."

They walked across the open space of the park, and through the woods. Snow had fallen in the night, and, here beyond the walls and hedges, it was a smooth fair sheet upon which had been scribbled the record of the night's activities of all the small things that lived in the wood. Here was the delicate tracery of the mice, with the thin line of a dragging tail etched between the footprints; here were the footsteps of the gray squirrels, two little prints and two big ones. There were paths trodden by the pheasants, as smooth-beaten as though the feet of men had walked on them and packed down the snow.

But what Mr. Bonaparte bade Hugh look for was the snowshoe-shaped groups of footprints made by the rabbits, bigger than the squirrels, the tracks of the hind feet marked deep where they pressed down for a long wide bound across the soft whiteness. Wherever there were thickets or fallen trees or hedges, Mr. Bonaparte had Hugh look thoroughly along them for the gaps through which the rabbits had found a runway, and had him examine each gap. In one of them Hugh found a snare of wire, set by some boy of the village who wanted rabbit stew for supper, or rabbit fur to line his winter cap.

Mr. Bonaparte had Hugh plunk it out and throw it away. "That is what I am seeking," he said. "Always I do this every winter, and will not let anybody do it for me. I do not like traps; I cannot bear to think of things as caught and held in captivity. And I have learned that it is in these little gaps that traps and snares are set. I know, too, that almost anywhere in the world, where there are woods and fields and rabbits, there are boys who will set traps for them."

They discovered a good many before they were done. In one snare a rabbit was caught, but Hugh managed to get him free without hurting him. In some places were boxes with spring lids, or a figure-four trap which would drop a box over the unwary rabbit who nibbled at the bait. These Mr. Bonaparte delighted in smashing with his hatchet. "I will not have it," he kept saying. "I will not have it."

They had walked through the whole circuit of the wood and now came out on the brow of the hill about Crosswicks Creek, the little stream which ran into the Delaware and made the high point of land on which the buildings of Point Breeze were set. There was a mass of thickets at the edge of the slope, the beginning of the close underbrush that ran down to the stream.

"You look at that end of the bushes; I will take this," Mr. Bonaparte said. "This is the last one we will have to search for traps." They separated and Hugh went to the far end of the straggling row of branches to lift the whips of bare stems and peer underneath. Mr. Bonaparte was busily beating and searching at his own end, so interested in what he was seeking that he paid no great heed to where he was going. Hugh rose from his stooping, and cried suddenly, "Take care, don't get too near the edge of the hill." Mr. Bonaparte had pressed in among some small trees, and, as he straightened up in his turn, a little startled at being so suddenly addressed, he stepped back, happened to tread on a strip of hard frozen snow and, without warning, plunged backward over the slope of the hill. The ground dropped far and steeply down to the water; there were sharp juttings of stone on the slope; there were stumps and broken trunks of trees. Hugh rushed after him, thinking over and over, "The hatchet, the hatchet in his hand!"

But very luckily the hatchet had flown from his grasp as he first fell, and Mr. Bonaparte had slid, struggling and floundering down the hill, but without it. Blackberry branches caught at his big coat; a broken tree trunk held him finally. Hugh had come coasting down after him; he flung himself forward now and just caught the edge of the fur coat as Mr. Bonaparte helped him to his feet. They stood a moment to get their breath, then set about climbing upward with Hugh dragging and guiding and breaking out the way.

They got to the top at last and Mr. Bonaparte stood still, while Hugh brushed the snow from him.

"That was not well done of me," Joseph Bonaparte said. "I should have heeded your warning. If you had not been so quick when I was caught against the tree trunk I would have slipped over the edge into the stream." A plunge through the thin ice on Crosswicks Creek would have been a serious matter on that cold day.

Hugh said only, "I am afraid the hatchet is not to be got back."

"No, we must leave it, I suppose," Bonaparte answered a little ruefully. He was a thrifty man and hated waste, but the snowdrifts had buried the hatchet and there was small use in looking for it until spring. The sun was dropping low above the river, and the air was still and chilly. It was time that they turned their faces toward home.

The distance was almost two miles, for the park extended far along the creek and the bluffs of the Delaware. They tramped along in silence for the most part, with Hugh a little ahead to plow through the deepest of the snow. The winter sunset was clear yellow before them; the call of quail was distinct in the quiet air and the wide expanse of white was empty.

Mr. Bonaparte broke the silence. That little experience on the hillside seemed to have brought the two into closer acquaintance, seemed to have set them on the common level of two human beings together. His eye swept the far circuit of the park, the woods, the hill above the river, and the bulk of the distant house, dark against the thin yellow of the sky. "It is a good place," he said, as though half to himself. "A fair and happy place. I wish he could see it now."

Hugh could guess well enough who was meant by that word "he." There were a number of sons in the Bonaparte family. Joseph, Lucien, Jerome—Jules had told him of all of them. But when Mr. Bonaparte spoke of "my brother," he referred to but one man, Napoleon. When he said "he," there was no question as to whom he meant.

Hugh knew better than to answer, for was he not the gardener's boy still? But Joseph Bonaparte was in the mood for talking, for opening his mind, as a man with a pent up secret will do, to someone who is not too close to him, who will listen and speak no word.

"He will see it," he cried out, "and it will not be long either. He will see it."

At this, Hugh, in his astonishment, could not keep from exclaiming. "He will see it? This place?"

Joseph Bonaparte seemed hardly to know who was speaking thus. "Once, long ago, when his enemies were pressing him close, I said to my brother, half in joke, that if the worst came, we could flee to America. There was a map on the table before him and he laid his finger upon it. 'I have thought of that,' he said. He had always thought of everything. 'If I should take refuge in America, I would choose this spot to live, part way between Philadelphia and New York, so that when ships came in at either port I should have the news at once.' And so, since I could not persuade him to come, I have found this place and live here—waiting for news of him."

They had come to a rough hollow and Hugh stepped back and steadied Mr. Bonaparte's arm. It was not so much that he needed help on the little slope, but that he needed the touch of some friendly person. Somehow Hugh knew that, while he must not speak or make comment, he could show, at least, what he felt. Joseph Bonaparte's voice had been excited, high, but now it dropped lower. "He will come back. I know he will come back. He escaped from the Island of Elba. Is the island of St. Helena, then, too far away?"

They had walked far, and the house was visible now through the trees, with lights coming out in the windows and the sky behind it growing dark. Joseph Bonaparte seemed to realize at last how much he had been saying to a gardener's boy, although he had, in truth, only been putting into words, for his own relief, the thoughts of which his mind was so full. But he had a question to ask. Hugh had expected it for a very long time.

"You have lived in France, boy. Did you ever see Napoleon?"

"Yes," Hugh told him. He described that day in Paris with the marching troops, the banners and the cheers, told how his father had taken him upon his shoulder so that he might look over the heads of the people and see the Emperor go by. But he remembered what Mr. Girard had said, and stopped when he got to the end of those few words, even though that second time that he had seen Napoleon was far clearer in his mind. And fortunately Mr. Bonaparte did not ask him further questions. They walked on together, passed through the garden and came up to the broad steps. Mr. Mailliard came hastily out of the door to meet them.

"Bodine thought that you had taken the carriage and gone into Trenton. I only this moment got back and found out, sir, that you were out here in the snow," he said. His tone was worried and he did not speak Bodine's name with any approval. The big doors were thrown open and the two went in.

"We destroyed, oh, a score of rabbit traps," Mr. Bonaparte was recounting happily as they went up the steps. But he gave Hugh a friendly, meaning nod, as he disappeared. It seemed to say, among other things, "Do not tell Mr. Mailliard that I slipped over the hill into a snowbank."

Hugh walked away homeward with the stars coming out in tiny pricks of light in the darkening sky. He had much to

think about, much to talk about to his mother, to Hilda—
to Jeremy when he should come home.

The winter went by. Hugh stood at the head of the
school, where he truly belonged; and in the end he came
to expect it of himself, and Hilda was able to relax her
watchfulness a little. Hilda always did well, but it would
have been impossible for her to surpass Hugh when he was
doing his best.

Thus a whole year passed, and another. Mr. Bonaparte
moved into Philadelphia in the cold weather, or went
south. Old Jules' rheumatism kept him a little more from
the work and Hugh did a greater amount than before.
Otherwise there was little change at Point Breeze. Month
by month came letters from Jeremy. Even Hugh could see
in them how his brother changed, how he was growing up
to be a real man of affairs in this life of business and law. It
seemed hard to believe, after all this time, that there could
be any possibility of Grandfather's affairs being settled
as they should be, but Jeremy kept saying, "You do not
know how the law can delay," and seemed always hopeful
himself.

Part of the time Jeremy worked in some of the offices
of those foreign agents who did business for Mr. Girard,
going back to Copenhagen as he was needed. One of the
larger lawsuits concerning Mr. Girard's ships was settled
and a small one of Grandfather's, but others were still
unfinished. Often Jeremy was in charge alone now, while
Mr. Greening attended to other matters. Then, when
Mr. Greening returned, Jeremy would go away for a few
weeks or months, since it was no longer necessary for

both of them to be present at the same time. During those intervals he even took ship and made brief voyages up and down the coast of France, of Spain, and even as far as Algiers in the Mediterranean. But it was never possible, so it seemed, to dare embark upon the long voyage to America, which could easily take three months for going and coming. There was too much of a chance that he would be suddenly needed while he was away.

It was in the second spring that Hilda had another of her good ideas. How long she had been thinking of it nobody could quite say, but she brought it forward without warning as she always did. She and Hugh and Grandfather had been taking a walk together up the hill and along the paths and terraces of the big house, closed and waiting for better times. Hilda was examining the brave green spears of snowdrops and crocus which were poking up here and there in the leaf-drifted flower beds.

"This was a beautiful garden once," Grandfather sighed, "but it was almost gone even while I still lived here, and since then there was no one to take care of it."

"Why shouldn't we take care of it now?" Hilda proposed suddenly. "Hugh knows so much more about gardening than he did, than any of us do, and he is bigger. He could work here instead of in our garden and I could help him when there is time. And you, Mr. Nicolls, could come up here with us and tell us how the things used to be."

Grandfather's face colored with pleasure. Perhaps he had once thought that he would never come back to that long white house with its fine view over the river, perhaps even before that he had given up hope that he could ever see the garden cared for again.

They began that very minute to plan and count and calculate what must be done. The next day they set to work in earnest. Hugh had, indeed, learned much from old Jules; he knew more about flowers now than any of the Storrs family. Moreover, he could work so much better and faster than before that he could easily accomplish all he wanted in the spare time that he used to give to the Storrs' garden. His mother came to help too, and before summer the garden showed promise of being really itself again. They carried great basketfuls of flowers to the market, and, on the day the President of the United States, Mr. Monroe, was to dine in state with Mr. Girard in Philadelphia, Hugh had the delight of carrying to him such sheaves of great pink roses that the whole house was filled with them. Mr. Girard called Hugh into his library to thank him.

By an unspoken agreement they had stopped talking together of any date for Jeremy's return, but Mr. Girard spoke of him now. "Your brother is learning much of world affairs," he said to Hugh. "This is, indeed, the beginning of his career, for it is plain from all accounts that he had a good head for this trade between nations, which is really what holds us all together as a peaceful world. Do not grudge him the time that is being granted him to learn so much of what he needs to know." And he added a question which must have been in his mind for some time. "That strange fellow whom you drove out of Mr. Bonaparte's apartments, the man for whom we searched through all the inns of Philadelphia, have you ever had a sight of him again?"

No, Hugh had not, though he had watched faithfully. He wondered how the stranger could have been so keen in his purpose for a little while and then given it up so completely.

Mr. Girard answered thoughtfully. "It was always probable that he was not there on his own account, but sent by someone, high at Court, who wanted to lay hands on the letters we have spoken of. And it is very possible that the person who sent him has been out of office or out of favor, as so often can happen for a year or two or even more. If such a courtier or officer should come into power again, then perhaps he will renew his efforts; for nothing would give a man such a hold on the gratitude of his King or Emperor or Czar as to restore those papers in which the rulers of Europe asked for favors, asked for mercy, from Napoleon Bonaparte. So watch carefully, my good Hugh. The time of his return may come yet."

Hugh had watched, and he watched even more carefully now. But again a summer passed with no signs of the young man who went, in some places at least, by the name of Dominic. It seemed, indeed, that he was gone forever. The winter came again, the snow fell, it was December, Christmas passed, and the new year was at hand. Hugh had one great anxiety—he had not heard, no one had heard, for many weeks from Jeremy. Hugh's mind was completely on that, but still occasionally he thought of Dominic vaguely, trying to imagine, if the fellow did come back, what would be the manner of his coming. Nothing, nothing that he could possibly have fancied, could have been anything like what it really turned out to be.

It was at the beginning of January, a cold, snowy day,
a Saturday, when Hugh was at Point Breeze to do some
special task for Madame Le Mar. A big painting had
to be taken down and cleaned, and she had so put her
trust in Hugh's carefulness that he was one of the few
chosen ones who was even allowed to touch one of the
great works of art. With the tallest footman, who had
also earned her confidence, the two were lifting the big
frame from its place on the wall in the main hallway. Mr.
Bonaparte was upstairs in his library, dictating to François
Bodine. Mr. Mailliard had gone to New York for a day or
two on business for Mr. Bonaparte. While he was away,
all his authority was in the hands of François Bodine.
Mr. Bonaparte had begun to write down his memories
of the Court of Spain, and was not to be disturbed. Mr.
Mailliard had long wanted him to make a book of all
he remembered, and, now Mr. Bonaparte had begun it,
was most anxious that nothing should interrupt him.
"No matter what happens, let Mr. Bodine settle it," Mr.
Mailliard had directed in Hugh's hearing. François Bodine
and Hugh had had little to do with each other for a very
long time. Hugh had learned by now just how to keep out
of his way, and certainly Bodine never went out of his to
seek out the gardener's boy.

Just as the picture had been carried away and Hugh was
putting up a small one to cover its place, there was a sound
of carriage wheels on the drive outside, steps on the porch,
and a knock at the door. It was opened, and a man with
bags and boxes stood on the threshold, a traveler, one of
those countless visitors who came and went at Point Breeze
for Mr. Bonaparte was fond of company and enjoyed

having guests. Hugh heard what the newcomer was saying, and stood still instantly. Could it be possible that he had heard that voice before?

"I have a letter of introduction to Mr. Bonaparte," the visitor was announcing, "from an old friend of his and of the Bonaparte family. I was given to understand that if I came here to present it, I might possibly stay a few days, to give Mr. Bonaparte—I should say the Comte de Survilliers—news of what is going on abroad. I have much to say to him that he might like to hear."

The footman who had opened the door hesitated a little. "Will you come inside, sir?" he said finally. "I will call Mr. Bodine, the secretary in charge, if you will be so good as to wait a few minutes."

"I am not used to being kept waiting," the stranger replied impatiently. "I am sure Monsieur le Comte will not like to have words wasted over the reception of someone who he wished to see." He moved his hand and there was a little chink as of money passing between him and the servant.

At this moment Mr. Bodine himself came down the stairs. He stood for a moment in talk with the stranger, seemed deeply impressed by the man's haughty manner and the letter with the red seals that he showed him, was moved perhaps even by that glint of gold which had plainly flashed from the guest's hand to the servant's.

"If you will come upstairs, I will present you to the Comte de Survilliers," he said. "He is, indeed, occupied for the moment, but I can show you to your room. I am sure he will be delighted to have you remain here as long as suits your pleasure." Many and many a time equally unknown guests had been received at Point Breeze on the strength of letters or messages from someone Mr. Bonaparte knew abroad.

The footman stooped to take up his bags and, led by Mr. Bodine, the stranger moved toward the stairs. It was then that he came at last full within Hugh's line of seeing. There could be no doubt of it; the voice had been almost unmistakable, the face and bearing were beyond any question. In spite of the elaborate green coat, the high stock, the careful dressing of his hair; in spite of the passing of two years which had made a youth of nineteen or so over into a man of the world of twenty-one—in spite of all these things still there could be no doubt. This guest presenting himself so boldly and being conducted so cordially up the stairs was no other than Dominic whom Hugh had once seen, fleeing in terror, plunging and leaping down to the safety of his boat at the edge of the Delaware.

For an instant Hugh stood motionless, hidden in the shadow at the turn of the corridor, watching the man mount upward. Then he dashed forward and cried out, "Mr. Bodine, Mr. Bodine!"

The secretary turned, scowled, but came back down the stairs while the guest walked on, with the footman behind him carrying his cloak and bags.

"What do you want?" Bodine demanded angrily. "What can you mean by interrupting me when I am welcoming His Excellency's guest?"

"But you should know. He is the one—the very one who

was here before," cried Hugh. "I have told you, I have told
Mr. Bonaparte. Mr Girard talked with you—of his spying,
his slipping in. This is the same man, after all this long
time. Don't—don't let him stay in this house."

Bodine's face was fiery red and his waiting anger burst
forth at last. "I have had enough of your suspicions of this
person or that, your foolishness, your impudence. Begone
from this house, from this place. We are finished with you.
Do you understand that? You are discharged from your
service here, and are not to come back again."

Hugh stood staring at him, dumb with astonishment.
"You can't discharge me—" he began, but Bodine
interrupted, more heated than ever. He put his hand into
his pocket and pulled out a handful of coins.

"Mailliard put matters into my hands. I had wished
from the first that I might use that power to get rid of you.
Now I have good and ample reason. There is your money.
You are to go."

He flung the silver on the little table, where Hugh let
it lie. The boy caught a glimpse of the footman standing
astonished and dismayed in the shadow of the passage.
Hugh turned away from the horrified staring of one man,
and the hot angry face of the other, and walked away down
the hall. Above him he heard the closing of a door, as the
visitor was ushered into the guestroom at the top of the
stairs.

CHAPTER 7

The Ship Superb

How many times Hugh had tramped that road and the lane which led between Point Breeze and the Storrs' house! But it had never seemed so long to him as on that afternoon, with the clouds hanging heavy above, the fields desolate, the trees bare and dismal in the raw weather of a snowless day of early January. His heart was so heavy that it seemed to make the way longer, the hollows deeper, the upward rises steeper. He wondered in just what words he would tell his mother and his grandfather and Hilda that his work at Point Breeze was over. He was tormented by a strange wish that he could have found time to walk out to the hillside and lay his hand, just for a minute, on the great trunk of the oak tree which he felt was his.

But he must not think of that; he must think what this news would mean at home. What they would do without his wages was rather a serious question. Nevertheless, as he went along in the chill weather, he began to think, instead, of the warm, cozy room where they all gathered in the evening, with the curtains drawn and the fire burning, the wooden armchairs, the table with its bright cloth, everything so simple and familiar, so blessed simply by being home. Point Breeze was not a home. It was—what was it? His mind began to work on that question and he forgot his own troubles. The low farmhouse came into view among the pointed poplars; he walked between the holly bushes bright with their red berries, opened the gate, crossed the garden, and came into the house.

The room was empty and still, with the fire sending shafts of moving light across it. He was glad for a minute to have no one to speak to, and to be able to sit down quietly and collect his thoughts a little. What was happening over yonder at Mr. Bonaparte's house? Was there anything more that he could, or should, do? Once more his mind began going round and round over the problems which he could not solve. He was very tired. He was sitting deep in Grandfather's chair, enjoying the warmth and the quiet, when Hilda came bursting in.

"Oh, Hugh, I have been waiting for you. How did you get home so early? There was a message, half an hour ago; a man on horseback stopped with word from Mr. Girard. He wanted you to come to Philadelphia on the night coach if you possibly could. But he did not say why."

Hugh jumped up. Mr. Girard's name had banished all his weariness. He ran upstairs two steps at a time to get his other coat. His mother was moving about in his room, gathering his things together, packing the small bag, laying out his dark, warm coat and the red muffler she had just finished knitting. She did not take time to make comment or to wonder over the message.

"We were so afraid you would not be in time," she said. "Hilda would have gone down to Point Breeze to get you if you had been delayed. Now you will really catch the coach."

Travel had increased along the New Jersey highways in two years, and there was a coach that passed through Bordentown every evening and made a night run into Philadelphia. Hard going it was, but it saved a vast amount of time. His mother repeated, "It is such good luck that you came home early."

He told her now how that had come about, that he was sent away from Point Breeze to return no more. He saw her thin cheeks flush with indignation when he spoke Bodine's name, but even now she did not waste time over discussion.

"It is lucky you came home early just the same. Certainly Mr. Girard must want you for something important. We will think about Point Breeze later."

There was not much more preparation and certainly there was very little more time. Hilda and her father had harnessed Dolly to the chaise; Hilda came running in to say they were ready to drive him back down the lane to the high road where the coach would pick him up. He said a hasty goodbye. He felt almost as important and useful as though he were Jeremy, going away by special summons from Mr. Girard. They spun away down the rutty lane, even Dolly partaking of the excitement and hurrying at her most bouncing trot. They got out where the lane met the public highway, and waited.

It was dark now and very cold. Hugh's teeth were chattering a little as he stood by the road. As they stood waiting, they began to realize that the wind was coming

up, harsh and cold, sweeping across the snow-covered
fields. Presently there was a rumble of wheels and the beat
of horses' feet in steady rhythm. The coach appeared, huge
and unreal in the darkness. It hardly seemed believable
that such a great, rolling thing would stop for so small a
figure as himself, Hugh Armond, waiting at the roadside.
But the coachman shouted to the horses, they drew up,
the big coach came to a standstill, and Hugh climbed up.
He waved his hand to Hilda, whom he could just make
out standing in the road. In no time at all they were
passing the gates of Point Breeze, the lights from the house
faintly visible beyond the trees of the park. How little it all
mattered to him now.

He had only the least anxiety, in the far corner of his
mind, as to what the stranger might be doing. Probably
he would be sitting down to dinner with Mr. Bonaparte in
the big dining room with its great chandelier of a hundred
wax candles. They would, no doubt, be talking of all the
great matters that were going on abroad, and, within his
scheming mind, the man would be shaping a plan by
which he could lay hands on what he had come to find.
Mr. Bonaparte would be affable and kind and polite, so
glad to see a stranger who could bring him news from so
far away. How little he would be dreaming of what was
going on in that handsome head across the table. Bodine
would be smiling uncomfortably; Bodine never seemed
to be at ease when he was in the presence of people whom
he considered his betters. But in his own mind François
Bodine would be pleased over what he had done that day.
He had gotten rid of Hugh Armond who had offended
him so long ago. Well, it did not matter to Hugh. He had

other affairs to attend to, even though he did not know just what they were. The coach whirled him away into the dark; Point Breeze was left behind and went completely out of his thoughts.

It was certainly not the most restful manner of spending the night to try to sleep even on the inside seat of a coach which pitched and tossed over the ruts and over the rises and dips of the road. The wind was rising steadily, and it was very cold. Finally the gale blew so heavily that on the stretches of road where the horses had to drive into it, the coachman had to talk, threaten with his whip, finally shout at them to be heard above the noise of the storm. The coach trembled like a ship. Across the flat fields of New Jersey the wind rose to high fury, screaming overhead, carrying a sparse flight of snow that stung and cut every face that turned toward it. There was an older man in the coach on the seat opposite Hugh, who slid down farther and farther into his great rough coat, but who never closed his eyes for a moment all night. He talked to Hugh a little. He was counting the hours, counting the miles, flinching as each fresh new gust swirled about the great clumsy vehicle. He had a wife ill in Philadelphia; he must get home to her—he kept saying it again and again, "I must, I must get there."

Hugh must have slept at last, for when he awoke it was gray morning and they were drawn up at the ferry landing. The wind was not at the same screaming height, but the whole surface of the river was dark and cut with choppy white-capped waves. A great argument was going on outside. The man who ran the ferry refused to cross in such weather. Hugh's anxious fellow passenger said that he had to. But the ferryman was not to be shaken.

"A big unwieldy boat like this would get crosswise of the waves and there'd be no doing anything with her," he insisted. "If you must be set over to the other side, I'll go ask Nels Hanson what he can do for you. Sometimes he takes folks across in his smaller boat when the ferry can't make it. But cross with the ferry I will not, even if the President of the United States asked me."

The search produced Nels Hanson, a yellow-haired Swede who seemed to have no fear of trying the voyage across in his little single-sailed boat. "She's weather wise; she can make it," he assured them calmly.

The other passengers on the coach were not so certain that he knew what was possible and what was impossible. But the man with the sick wife was bound to cross. "If you care to, you can try it with me, boy," he said. Hugh was quite ready to go.

He thought he was used to bad weather, but it was only on the sea that he had seen it. There was something entirely different about the choppy, vicious waves of a river, slapping against the banks and backing off to entangle themselves with others. They tossed and pitched the little sailboat, but the wind was high and steady and carried them in one furious sweep from one bank to the other. Fog or snow hung low over the wide Delaware, so that it was not possible to see more than a hundred yards away. There was little danger of running into anything, however, for there were few craft, indeed, abroad on the river on such a morning. When they got to land, a messenger was still waiting for Hugh's fellow passenger. It was so early still, so dark and foggy, that he was carrying a lantern. "She's better," the servingman said. "They sent me to tell you the minute you landed. But it's good you've come, sir."

Hugh tried to thank him, but the anxious gentleman only nodded and made haste to the cabriolet that was waiting. Hugh set off along the dark, wind-swept streets, with the snow driving straight into his face as he went. He was so much more used to seeing Philadelphia green and quiet and serene. It was odd to see the snow whirled over the doorsteps, and most of the windows shuttered against the beating storm. Perhaps no one would be up at Mr. Girard's offices; he would have to wait in the street until somebody unbarred the doors.

But the door opened to his hand and, when he came in, a sleepy clerk got down from a stool and said at once, "Mr. Girard wishes you to come straight in, Mr. Armond." It was the first time Hugh had been called just that, in the place. It made him feel more like Jeremy than ever. The young man opened the inner door, and spoke Hugh's name. Hugh went in.

There was a roaring fire on the white marble hearth and the room was bright with the flickering flame. Hugh noticed, however, that the candles on the desk were guttered and burned short, as were those upon the mantel. Mr. Girard laid down a paper and turned round to greet him. His face was gray and tight drawn, with the look that every man has when he has been up all night.

"You got here in good time," he said. "I was in fear that you could not cross the river."

"The boat pitched a good deal," Hugh admitted. Only now did he realize that they had been in real danger. He had sat down in the chair to which Mr. Girard motioned him, but he looked across into this friend's face. "You have not slept; you have been here all night," he said.

Stephen Girard nodded. "Yes, I have a ship in the Delaware, the Superb. I have been waiting all night for her to signal that she is abreast of the wharf."

Hugh stood up. The thought which had come to him was one which could not be met except upon his feet. "A ship—do you mean . . ."

Girard nodded. "I have reason to believe that Thomas Greening and Jeremy Armond sailed on her from Liverpool five weeks ago. I cannot be certain, for no swifter vessel has come in ahead of this one. But I was sure enough of it to send for you. When I dispatched my messenger, I had no idea that this storm would delay our knowing. She is many hours overdue, but I get word from time to time as to her progress up the river. The wind and tide have been against her, but in half an hour the tide will turn and should bring her in." As Hugh swung about toward the door, he held up his hand. "One does no good, boy, by standing on the wharf and trying to bring her in by strength of will. I have tried it a hundred times. It is fairer to those who are struggling against wind and tide not to watch as the chance of fortune goes up and down for them."

Hugh sat down again, and tried to wait. The two of them could not talk; the only sound in the room was that of the fluttering banners of flame in the deep chimney place.

How often, Hugh wondered, had Mr. Girard sat in that same room, facing those same anxieties and dreads, facing them with a calm face but most surely with a tumult within his heart? He had lost ships by war and by storm and by piracy, but still he sent them out, still he sat and waited with that drawn, quiet face for them to come home again. He guessed Hugh's thought, for he smiled across at him.

"I lost my first ship when the British took it, when they occupied Philadelphia in the war of the Revolution. As they departed, they took the Betsey with them. But I got others. I have lost them too, but many times they came home to me with cargoes valuable beyond my expectation, many a time they have gone out with goods on board that were above price—American grain and foodstuffs which met the desperate needs of famine-ridden countries. The British took my first one; the wind will take my last, but I shall go on sending them out and welcoming them home, as long as there is breath within me." They sat silent for a long time. Then the clerk from the other room put his head in at the door.

"It's growing lighter, sir. The wind is bad, but not as fierce as it was. The last messenger said they could make out her shape through the snow, that she's rounding in and dropping anchor."

At that, Hugh was up and out of the room, out of the building and down the street. He ran along the docks. Only here and there was a snow-wrapped dockman crouched in the shelter of a building, trying to peer through the driving flakes. One of them pointed. "She's there, the Superb. She's like a ghost, but I can make her out.

I heard the splash of her anchor. I think they are lowering a boat."

When the wind dropped for a moment's lull, it was possible to hear the creak of oarlocks. There was a scraping sound as the bow of a boat touched the wharf. Hugh, wind whipped and shrouded in snow, darted forward as two tall figures rose from the stern. Jeremy Armond was the first one on shore.

It was a long counsel that was held in Mr. Girard's office that stormy morning. Hugh watched and listened from his corner by the fireplace, while the men talked, while breakfast was brought in, while papers were piled high on the table. Although Thomas Greening and the captain of the Superb were present, Jeremy Armond seemed to be the one appointed to give the report of how the work was successfully completed; of how Hiram Nicolls and Stephen Girard had each recovered one ship and the value of the others. There was something in Jeremy's quick, ready speech which made the tale so clear that the others left the telling of it mostly to him. What an account it was, of long waits, of patience, of bold courage in demanding what was the American right, of waiting again until minds of a different sort had ample time to think the matter over.

"Some men who had been making profit out of the seizing of ships fought us every inch of the way," Jeremy recounted. "But the Danes are just; it was finally proved that the ships should not have been taken and then, one by one, the judgements were given in our favor. But it took a long time, a very long time."

Mr. Thomas Greening spoke up in his turn. "I would

have lost patience a hundred times and lost my temper, too, if the truth be told. But this boy has a real gift for such matters; he held his tongue and held to the task, when I would have cast it aside as impossible and beyond any man's bearing to wait and try and reason and argue for so long."

Jeremy smiled across at his brother. "I could not have borne it either, had there not been some change, now and again. I had the journey into Switzerland with Mr. Mailliard. But the best part of that expedition, even better than the great minute of digging in the fox hole and hearing the spade strike iron, better far than that was hearing about Hugh and all that he was doing at Point Breeze." Mr. Girard in his turn looked across at Hugh and smiled approval.

"You could have heard far more than Mailliard could ever have taken time to tell you," he told Jeremy. "It has been necessary for you to show much patience and willingness to wait long, but think what waiting your younger brother has done. He has acquitted himself well; he has given stout aid to his own household and that of Mr. Bonaparte. And he has never lost heart."

He pushed back his chair and put the papers together. "It takes youth to carry through these difficult accomplish-ments," he said. "The young do not lose hope. And now," he concluded, "I have not done with you, for we must go over to the bank and gather together some gentlemen who have been concerned with me in this matter, and give to them your report. Therefore you are to stay in Philadelphia until tomorrow, if you will, Jeremy Armond, and I will need Hugh also to carry messages to those who should come to hear the account of all that has happened. My own clerks will be burst every moment with all the accounts and invoices that the return of the Superb has brought." He glanced up at the clock and added suddenly, "Though I need you both until tomorrow, Hugh had better scurry off to the inn whence the coach starts, and have the coachman carry word to Bordentown that the ship Superb and Monsieur Jeremy Armond are arrived safely from overseas." He called a clerk. "Give the younger Monsieur Armond a list of those who had interest in the ships captured at Copenhagen," he said. "He can carry the messages to them after he has stopped to speak about the coach."

While the clerk set down the names, and Hugh stood by his desk waiting, he heard the talk still going on in the inner room. Mr. Girard was asking one more question. "There is one thing I do not understand. We had reports from you regularly, but just before your return there was no letter for three, perhaps it was four, months."

Jeremy replied. "There seemed to be a long time to wait, as there was ever and again, so I left Copenhagen to look for a place as clerk on a short voyage. I had done that same thing before, usually on the English ships of the East India Company. They would carry me to Gibraltar or Lisbon and I would take another to come back, attending to the Company's papers on board. So I took a berth on the Calcutta, thinking to be back again in a few weeks. But she put to sea under sealed orders and when the captain opened them we found the voyage was to be a different one, and I had no chance to make a short journey of it."

"And where did the ship take you?" Girard asked.

Hugh heard his brother draw a deep breath before he answered. "She was carrying dispatches to St. Helena, sir." he said.

The clerk just then handed Hugh the list and, if he were to get word to the coach, he must be off. He could ask Jeremy about that voyage later; there would be time now, all the time in the world. He opened the door and was off. The snow had ceased to fall, but the streets were white and silent with it. The rattle of carts on the rough cobbles was hushed and the horses plodded along on muffled feet. He found to his dismay that the coach had set off earlier than its proper time, and that, therefore, he could not send word home of Jeremy's arrival. The two boys would have to bring the news themselves.

It was early in the afternoon that the meeting took place within the great columned building of Mr. Girard's bank. Hugh helped in the long room where the merchants gathered, one among them being his old acquaintance of the post chaise, Mr. James Anthony. Hugh was sent back and forth to bring pens and papers, to ask for lists and invoices from the clerks outside. He heard Jeremy give his account, clearly and briefly. Mr. Thomas Greening gave added explanations at the end, and a long discussion followed, for Mr. Anthony had much to ask and to say. Hugh lost interest and slipped from the room to wait outside.

A clerk whom he knew took him on a tour through the bank, showed him the vaults and the great locks and the

heaps of gold and silver piled up for the next day's needs.
He was a gray-haired man, old in the service of Stephen
Girard. In one of the rooms in the cellar he showed Hugh
a great chest of iron, as big as one of the trunks with
which Mr. Bonaparte went traveling to Saratoga in the
summer, and they were large indeed. He put a key into
the complicated lock and opened the cover. Within were
jewels, in boxes, in bags, in metal caskets, rubies and
sapphires and diamonds by the basketful.

"I have to go through them now and again," the clerk
said. "Mr. Girard once happened to say that he would
like you to see them when there was a chance. Here is the
collection which Mr. Mailliard and your brother went to
get in Switzerland, although Mr. Bonaparte has taken away
a good many of the stones. He bought some land, north of
New York, and paid for it, they say, directly in diamonds."

"But who owns the others? Does Mr. Girard?" Hugh
asked, for there were scores and heaps of shining gems,
besides necklaces and rings and bracelets that shimmered
in the light of the candles they were carrying.

"No, Mr. Girard owns none of them. But for years
people have been sending him such things to keep. When
the French wars reached the West Indies, and when,
also, there was a rebellion of slaves there, then the rich
landowners, fearing the jewels would be taken from them,
sent them by Mr. Girard's captains to be carried to him.
Even before he had the bank, this great chest stood in his
own strong room, filled with all his wealth of precious
stones. Long before he had much money in his own, he
had in his hands these valuables of others to the amount of

a dozen fortunes. People have always had a way of trusting Mr. Girard."

When the meeting was over, it was arranged that the two boys should take the night coach for Bordentown. "You will get there by coach more quickly than I could take you in my chaise," Stephen Girard said, "even though it is my intention to make the journey tomorrow. I have things to talk over with your grandfather and also with Mr. Bonaparte. But I could not reach there before afternoon and it is wrong to let your mother wait one more hour than she should, to have you at home again."

They had supper in the rooms of old Mrs. Duane, for the place was close to the inn whence the coach started. They sat in George Washington's stately apartment, but they talked little of the past, only of the exciting future. Mrs. Duane rattled on in continuous flow of talk, mostly concerning Mr. Girard; it was remarkable how much she could say and still never delay one moment in making the supper ready and serving them. It was a gusty evening and she buttoned each boy up to the neck with her own hands, to make sure that he had enough scarves and mufflers and that they were well tucked in. The boys made their way through the gathering dark to the innyard. Only a few people were gathered there, since not many travelers cared to brave the cold and the jolting of a journey on such a night as this. But it was no such terrifying weather as that which had gone with them on the night before.

The landlady of the inn made her husband bring out extra blankets and rugs, and give each passenger a stone jug of hot water to nurse between his feet. "You'll be glad of them before morning," she said, when the men smiled a little at her carefulness. "They can be filled up again where you stop to bait the horses. I've heard tell that the snow is drifted deep across the New Jersey roads, and it may be noon before you get to Bordentown."

The dusk was just falling as they crossed on the ferry. Hugh could look down the river and see the ship Superb, warped in at the dock now, her tall masts towering so straight and high above the roofs of the warehouses, a throng of men like ants swarming over her decks unloading her cargo. His heart warmed to her—she was like no other vessel; she was the ship which had brought his brother home.

They would have much to talk of, and there would be plenty of time along the way. The other two inside passengers fell fast asleep immediately, so that it was as though they were alone. Hugh was overflowing with questions, but Jeremy would not listen to them, he wished to ask so many of his own. "This work of yours at the place of Mr. Bonaparte, just exactly what was it like?" he began. It was then and only then that the dismaying memory came to Hugh.

"Why, I had forgotten all about it, but I have been sent away; I am not to work there anymore. Oh, I never thought of it again, from the minute I saw the ship coming in. What are we to do?"

But that need not trouble him now, Jeremy reminded him of that. Grandfather had got back his own. Grandfather would be returning to his house, and Hugh would have all his time for school and for other things that he might like better. He would not need to worry about Mr. Bonaparte, and about the man who had discharged him. They were at the end of all that.

It was strange what a sudden and overpowering relief that idea was to Hugh. They were safe; they were all safe with each other again. The thought flowed over him in a tide of warm comfort. He realized, all at once, how very weary he was. Of course, he must stay awake. He told Jeremy a little, stumblingly, about Dominic and Bodine and the reasons why he had been discharged. But his mind was full of this wonderful new thought that the hard struggle was at an end! He fell asleep against Jeremy's shoulder.

It seemed as though no boy had ever slept so heavily. Jeremy had to shake him when they stopped at Moorestown and went into the inn for food and warmth and a little rest for passengers and horses. The news of the roads that they had heard in Philadelphia had been right; it was long after midnight when they reached the place where they should have been at nine o'clock. They refilled the jugs of hot water, glad of them indeed, for the night was bitter cold. It was daybreak when they got to Burlington, and the horses were changed. Even the fresh ones were soon worn out with pushing through the snow. Hugh was sleepy no longer now, as they rolled along the highway toward Bordentown. He and Jeremy were silent; the other passengers were awake, and they did not care to talk over their affairs too fully in the hearing of strangers. Hugh said at last:

"We are getting near Point Breeze. Watch for the big

gates. Do you remember? You only get one little glimpse of the house as you go by."

The gates were near. Jeremy leaned forward to look. But Hugh, as they came just opposite the long avenue gave a wild, excited cry. There was the house, half hidden behind the trees, and there—Could it be true? Yes, there could be no mistaking—there was a column of smoke and flame going up from the roof, fanned by the gusts of wind that blew in from the river.

The coachman drew up; he had seen it too. Everyone in the coach came tumbling out. Hugh tugged at the gates, but they were locked and the man who should have tended them had run up to the house. He slipped in through the little opening next to the lodge and dashed up the drive. Halfway down he met a flying figure, François Bodine, hatless, his coat scorched, his eyes wild. "Mr. Mailliard is not here," he cried. "And Mr. Bonaparte is not here. What am I to do? What are we to do?"

Jeremy was beside Hugh now, the passengers from the coach were pushing through the little gate, the coachman was getting down from his box. It was Jeremy who called up to him. "Don't get down. Whip up your horses and go into Bordentown for help. Spread the alarm as you go. Get word to Mr. Bonaparte."

Mr. Bodine recovered his wits a little, took out a key, and let the boys open the gates wide.

Then Hugh ran, outstripping Bodine and the rest, ran toward the house where the black-edged licking flames were creeping over the roof, sending up dense columns of dark and white smoke into the cold, windy air.

CHAPTER 8

Voyage to St. Helena

A burly coachman with four horses at full gallop is a swift and startling messenger, and there is no message which draws forth such instant response as the cry of fire. The whole of Bordentown, every inhabitant of the comfortable red brick houses which came almost up to the boundaries of Point Breeze, came pouring through the gates to offer help.

It was the women who arrived first. The men were at their work, in their offices, farther away than their wives and sisters doing the tasks at home. These left the bread to scorch in the oven, and the wash trailing out of the tubs, as they picked up their flounces and ballooning skirts and ran. They picked up something else. In every house it was required by law that a certain number of fire buckets should be kept, bright-painted leather receptacles, which, when an alarm of fire ran through the town, were to be thrown out into the street for the use of volunteer firemen. Every woman had two or three hanging from her arm; the children came running at their heels with the rest. It was a man's task to fill and carry them, but until the men could come the women and the children formed in lines from the well, from the pool in the garden. They filled the buckets, passed them from hand to hand, emptied them on the fire and swung them back down the line to be filled again. But bold and willing as they were, it was a feeble effort to pit against that devouring peril which stood straddling on the roof and breathed flame upward to the sky.

Hugh saw Madame Le Mar at the big front doors, closing them to keep back the draft of air that was rushing through the house and fanning the fire. "We can only hope to keep the flames back while we get things out," she said. "Bid everyone who has not a bucket to come in and fetch what can be moved. Take the busts of Napoleon first."

Jeremy was at Hugh's heels and the four passengers from the coach were close behind them. The stoutest gentleman seized a marble likeness of the Emperor in his arms and bore it out through the side door. Madame Le Mar, who could grow excited to the point of tears over the matter of house cleaning or a dinner party, was quite calm and steady now. She stood giving orders. "Napoleon first, if you please, sirs. Napoleon first. That is what Mr. Bonaparte would say."

The busts, the statues were lifted from their pedestals; the great battle pictures and the portraits came down from the walls and went plunging and staggering out through the side entrances or the long windows. Hugh took one moment to ask a question of one of the men servants.

"How did it happen? How did the fire start?"

"We do not quite know. It was in the room of Monsieur Dominic, the guest who came day before yesterday. He had locked his room and, so he said, had set off on an errand to the village. Perhaps sparks snapped from his fire; we could not get into the room and presently when Madame Le Mar passed in the corridor she smelt smoke and bade us come and break the door in. The whole place was ablaze."

The men of Bordentown had come by now: there were a hundred or more toiling, straining, taking orders, pushing in and out. Hugh saw the Storrs' chaise, with old Dolly galloping in the shafts, as it came up the drive. John Storrs, Hugh's mother, Mrs. Storrs, and Hilda all came tumbling out. And a moment after, a carriage with wildly dashing horses rattled up the road. It was Mr. Bonaparte coming home from Trenton, with Mr. Mailliard beside him.

Hugh had his own idea about what was to be done. He raced up the little side staircase and pushed into the upstairs library. Here, he knew, all the most precious valuables were kept in their locked cabinets between the bookcases. He did not know in which ones the letters were. He tried to wrench open the first of the doors, found the lock and the wood too strong for him and went dashing back to find Mr. Bodine and the keys. Through the whole of the second floor drifted the blinding smoke, and the air was almost too hot and heavy for breathing. At the opposite end one or two brave spirits had come up the stairway with buckets to throw water on the walls and hangings, but had been driven back. There was no hope of conquering the fire here. The central part of the house, being of wood, was a seething furnace, but the wings were brick, and the library was at the end of the wing. The fire would be slower here; there might be time to carry everything away. If only he could lay hands on Mr. Bodine.

When he did find him, he was in an argument with the Mayor of Bordentown as to whether the great picture of Napoleon crossing the Alps could be got down from the wall. Mr. Bodine thought not and wanted all efforts turned to something else, while the Mayor and his four stout companions calmly went on, tugging and shoving and jerking, to wrench the big painting from its place.

"The keys," Hugh cried into Bodine's ear. "The keys for the cabinets in the library."

"What keys?" Bodine returned. He seemed stunned, unable to take in what anyone said to him and kept repeating, "Get out of my way; you are hindering me. Why don't they try to get the carpets up instead of tearing at that picture? Why does no one pay attention to what I say?"

Hugh looked around in despair. Then he saw Mr. Mailliard stepping in at the long window. Mr. Bonaparte was behind him, but it was the secretary who came first. Hugh rushed up to him. "Upstairs—the library—there will be time—if we can get the cupboards open, but they are all locked."

Mr. Mailliard nodded quietly. "I have keys," he said. "Get half a dozen helpers, men to be trusted. We will save what we can."

Hugh had lost sight of Jeremy, but he saw him, now, dripping with water, for he had climbed up to the roof to empty pail after pail across the shingles, but had been driven back down the ladders as the fire ate its way toward the wing. Hugh beckoned three others. They went up the side stairs again and into the stifling smoke-filled room.

The room was not empty. There was somebody already there, half hidden in the smoke, wrenching at one cupboard door after another—a tall, thin, black-haired fellow in a dark green coat. "Dominic," Hugh cried. The other turned at the sound of his voice. "That is he, the man I told you of," Hugh said to Jeremy, but instantly the fellow disappeared.

Mailliard unlocked one door after another, pulled out the shallow drawers and piled them up in the arms of those waiting to carry them out. With Hugh and Jeremy, he pressed as far down the room as he could. But none of them could get to the further end, for the fire was sweeping into Mr. Bonaparte's dressing room, and heat and flames were seeping through the door. One man made a raid upon the bedroom and came out with his arms full of waistcoats, silk shirts, polished boots and trailing coats, but no one could try it again.

Nor was it possible to reach the cabinet drawers at the far end of the room beyond the fireplace. They could only seize what was within reach and carry away the drawers with their medals, cases of jewels, gold snuff boxes, miniatures with their frames set with diamonds, the hilt of a sword studded with gems. They were all brought out and borne away. Hugh saw Jeremy fill his arms with books, whose gold-tooled binding were too beautiful to leave for the fire to devour. The room grew hotter and closer; the fire roared and raged beyond the farther wall. Suddenly the door of Mr. Bonaparte's bedroom burst open under pressure of flame, reached into the room, vanished and then flung itself out again.

The door of a cupboard dropped from its hinges; the fire had been charring inside, and now, in the hot draft, a swirl of half-burned papers, their edges black and ragged, came streaming out into the room. Hugh picked up one of them. Jeremy had carried the books to safety and had come back. He looked rapidly about, for this was their last moment. "There, on the mantel," Hugh directed; his own arms were full. Jeremy snatched a little portrait of Napoleon, painted on ivory, with sapphires set all around it, a picture of the Emperor when he was a boy. It was Napoleon first, it was Napoleon last, for they stumbled down the stairs together and the flames swept into the room. A crash above told that the roof was beginning to fall.

Outside, the crowd had dropped back. There was no use in filling the leather buckets anymore, although the lines had been extended all the way to the river and the water, poured everywhere, had made it possible to save most of the tapestries, rugs, silver, and paintings on the lower floor. But there was nothing to do now but to move back and see the house burn. Joseph Bonaparte, with Mailliard beside him, stood at a little distance, staring silently at the flames. He had seen fire and destruction before. There was no one who had followed the fortunes of Napoleon who had not become familiar with that. His hat was pulled low and the collar of his greatcoat was turned high against the biting wind behind him. He stood quite silent.

Jeremy spoke low. "That fellow that we saw upstairs when we first came in, we ought to look for him," he said. Hugh nodded. They threaded their way here and there through the crowd, but could catch no sight of him. All were standing with upturned faces staring at the fire and seeing nothing else. Round at the back of the house, however, there was no one, for the wind was blowing high and outward toward the river and carrying the smoke and sparks that way.

Then they saw him. He had sheltered himself from the wind and the hot blast behind the trunk of the big oak tree, and stood looking upward at the house. The framework of the main roof was bare now, showing the blazing beams and rafters; one of the big chimneys seemed to be toppling to its fall. So absorbed was the man in watching, and so sure, apparently, that no one was seeking him, that he did not notice the two until they had stolen close. He leaped back, but they were upon him, and had caught him by the arms. He struggled hard against them, bent and twisted, and flung them this way and that, but the two Armonds were strong and supple and he could not shake them off. At last he stood still, held between them, his breath coming short. Hugh, looking into his white face, saw again how young he was. For all the pretense of being a man, he was hardly more than a boy still. He spoke suddenly.

"I did not want to do it," he cried. "You may think what you will of me, but this is the truth. They made me do it. They forced me, these men who stood high in the court and wanted above everything else to hold the favor of the Czar. They had accused my father of treason against the Russian Crown—that was so easy to do in that troubled time after the wars with Napoleon. He was old, he could die if he were not released." He made a sudden plunging effort to get free, but it was no use. He spoke again.

"They told me I could buy his freedom if I would get the letters back which the Czar and the other Princes of Europe had written to Napoleon, in which they had begged mercy of him. I had been to America, I could speak English easily, I had been once to Bordentown—that was why they thought I could accomplish it, to get the letters back. I tried once and then told them it was impossible, and one of them had pity and freed my father. But they would not give it up. They sent me again; they made threats against my father once more, so that if I were to save him I must accomplish this. I could not get the letters, but I have made it so that no man can ever have them. That was all I could do."

His face was working; it was not with terror, but with some deeper feeling still. He added in a voice that did not sound like that in which he had spoken before, "The soldiers of Napoleon, when they marched through Russia, they burned my father's house. I can just remember, the big plain with snow on it, and the villages blazing as far as we could see. This is only one fire; then there were hundreds. But it was not for that I burned this house—it was to win my father's freedom. I can go back and tell them the letters are destroyed."

"Will they believe you?" Jeremy asked bluntly.

"Yes," he answered, "they must believe me. Let me move my arm a little, and I will show you."

Hugh loosed his grasp, though warily, and Dominic put his hand in his pocket. He, too, had picked up one of those half-burned scraps of paper. He held it up for them to look at in the red light of the fire. It was a blackened fragment, with a name scrawled across it which neither of the boys could make out; but there was a red seal in the corner, with an eagle on it and a crown. As they bent to look at it, suddenly Dominic twisted himself free, flung away from them and dashed toward the clump of trees beyond the summerhouse. They ran, but he was fleeter of foot than they. They called aloud for help, but the wind and the roar of the flames swept away the sound of their voices. This time the frozen river was no help to him; but he had evidently left a horse hidden, knowing it would be needed in haste. He flung himself into the saddle and was off like an arrow across the park toward the gate.

"Stop him, stop him," shouted both the boys together.

There were men in plenty to stop him or to pursue him, but at that moment the rafters began to crumble and drop into the furnace of flames below, the chimney slanted and lurched and went crashing down in a great shower of bricks and stones. No one heard, no one heeded the shouts of two boys or the galloping of a horse down the avenue. When the smoke had cleared and the people could look at one another again, the man had gone. Hugh drew a long breath.

"There's Mother over there," he said. In the rush of rapid excitement, Jeremy had not yet talked to her. They forgot the burning house; they forgot Mr. Bonaparte standing speechless in the little group beyond. They hurried across the frozen grass to tell Eleanor Armond that her son had come home.

The boys were both so cold and wet that their mother

said they must come at once to some place where they could be dried. They all climbed into the chaise somehow and, guided by Hilda, they made their way to the Bordentown Arms, where they could borrow some dry clothes, could toast themselves by the fire and be plied with hot drinks. Hilda and her father went on with Dolly to carry the great news of Jeremy's return to Grandfather; but Eleanor Armond would not let the two boys go on until they were thoroughly warm and dry. So they sat before the inn fire, these three who had not been together for so long, so unbelievably long. There was so much to tell that it was late afternoon before any one of the three thought of anything else but their own affairs. It was their mother who came first to the knowledge that there were other matters to think of than the sea voyage safely ended.

"You will want to go back to find out how Mr. Bonaparte is faring and see whether you can be of any further help to him," she said. "I will find someone to drive me home, and later you can come back to the Storrs' house when you are ready."

The two boys made their way through the gate of Point Breeze and across the park. The ruins of the house were still smoking but there was no glow of fire left. A crowd of people moved and chattered all about the place. On the driveway stood a traveling chaise with four horses. "It is Mr. Girard's," Hugh said.

Stephen Girard was with Joseph Bonaparte who had taken shelter in the gardener's cottage. Mr. Bonaparte was sitting in the little room, with a roaring fire going up the chimney and with his friend Stephen Girard in the wooden chair opposite. Outside, big wagons had been driven from the town and, under the directions of Mailliard and Bodine, the larger valuables, the marble figures, and the paintings were being loaded into them. Friends of Mr. Bonaparte had all offered to take them in until he should have a place to put them again. But in Jules' little house the smaller possessions were being gathered. One person after another would come in with a bag or a box or a handful of knickknacks which he himself had saved from the fire. Mr. Sarrett, the Mayor of Bordentown, was standing respectfully by the door, keeping count and tally of all that was brought in. The table was covered, drawers and boxes were piled up on the floor, everywhere that an inch of room could be found. Still they came pouring in—medals, jewels, ivory statuettes, all the contents of drawers and cupboards that it had been possible to carry away.

Mr. Bonaparte roused himself to give courteous thanks over and over again. "I am so grateful to you, merci, merci. With what kind neighbors I am surrounded. I did not know that people whose faces I have never seen could all treat me as a friend." There was a lull in the crowding at the door, a moment when the room was almost empty, in which he spoke across to Stephen Girard. "Do you see how great is the value of everything they have returned? Nothing touched, so far as I can see, not a single thing missing. It is wonderful."

"Not wonderful at all, sir." The voice of the Mayor spoke abruptly from the door. His tone was a trifle offended; he was bound to put the French gentlemen right. "You need not make a marvel of common honesty, Mr. Bonaparte.

Of course, none of these people would touch anything of yours, when they came to help you in your misfortunes."

Mr. Bonaparte was never at a loss for the polite and proper word, and he made haste to soothe Mr. Sarrett. The good Mayor was quite appeased at last, and all smiles again. Since no more people came in, he bowed and said goodnight. Mr. Girard glanced at the two boys, waiting at the door for a chance to speak, but Joseph Bonaparte did not seem to notice them. His face and manner were calm, but Hugh and Jeremy could see how he was knitting his hands together.

"I think—I keep thinking—my mind will turn to nothing else but this one thing, that I thought my brother was to see this house, to come to me someday. And now—what shelter do I have to offer him?" Mr. Girard sat looking at him long and thoughtfully. Then he turned his head, and with a nod summoned the two boys from the place where they had been waiting by the door. The room was empty now save for these four.

"I wish to present to you," Stephen Girard said, "a young friend of mine for whom I have the greatest respect and regard. You already know his brother, Hugh Armond, and should regard him no less. This is Jeremy Armond, who has been engaged in business overseas. He has just come back from Denmark and England. But before he returned he made a voyage—to the southward. The voyage was to St. Helena."

There was complete silence. Joseph Bonaparte raised his eyes to Jeremy's face and stared at him steadily and questioningly. Jeremy stood beside the mantel, thin, quiet, waiting at his ease. It was Mr. Bonaparte who was struggling for words, who got them out at last.

"And did you see the Emperor? Did you see his very face?"

Jeremy bowed his head. "Yes," he said. "I saw him. I talked with him."

"Did they permit you that?" cried Mr. Bonaparte sharply. "Those men who guard him—usually they have not allowed him to speak with strangers."

"They granted him that," Jeremy declared. "Word had got to him somehow that I was from New Jersey, from Bordentown. He begged that he might send you a message of affection, and they permitted it. He said I was to give you his love and deep affection, that you were never to forget all that had passed between two brothers."

"Was that all?" Joseph Bonaparte demanded. "No, there must have been something more. Did he send no word of what I was to expect, what I was to hope for?"

"He, himself, said nothing else, but I had other word to bring you. There is a man who loves and serves Napoleon, as Mr. Mailliard serves you; he is closer to him than any other. It was he who took me outside and, as we walked up and down the sea wall together, he also told me something that I was to tell you. He said . . ."

Jeremy hesitated. He glanced across at Mr. Girard, as though he could not continue. Mr. Girard had been looking into the fire but he raised his head. "Yes, go on," he directed Jeremy. "The truth may seem hard, but it is only the truth that will serve us now. If you have given him one message, you must give him the other."

"He said," Jeremy found his voice again, "this man said that—that you were to wait for your brother no longer, or for news of him. They know—all of them know; the Emperor himself knows—that he will never come back to rule France again. That was all. I was to repeat that to you, to say again that you were not to look for other news of him."

Mr. Bonaparte had sunk in his chair, looking little and old and shrunken. "That this should be the end," he whispered. "After such glory, after such glory!"

Jeremy put his hand in his pocket and took out the little picture, the last thing that had been rescued from the house, the portrait of the young Napoleon, thin-faced, dark, bold, mysterious, where it stood all alone, where the light of the fire, dancing on the wall opposite, was reflected again in the jewels of the frame.

As the two boys turned to the door to go, the master of Point Breeze, with a great effort, mustered the courtesy which, according to his idea, must always dwell in one who had been a king. He managed to say, "Thank you. I thank you greatly, my young friend." He bowed his head with grave dignity and then turned again to sit staring at the fire.

Stephen Girard got up and went out with them. "He is better to be alone for a little," he said, as he closed the door behind them. "There is nothing any man can say to make the truth easier to bear. Afterward it will be possible to offer him some comfort. But it was necessary that the whole world should understand at last that Napoleon will never return."

The afternoon had grown colder, but the skies were very clear. They had walked past the corner of the ruined house and could look out over the river, which was a smooth sheet of ice now, could see the ridge on the farther bank and the clump of trees which had once sheltered the plain, serene house of William Penn. There a very great man had worked and hoped and labored, and had not worked in vain. As the three stood looking at the ruins of Joseph Bonaparte's house, the same thought was shaping itself in the mind of each one of them, but Stephen Girard alone was able to put it into words.

"William Penn can never be forgotten, as long as men love liberty. And people talk of George Washington as though he had walked the streets of Philadelphia only yesterday. All men will talk of Napoleon, but they will not speak of him as they speak of these." They had moved a little farther, and now he looked up at Hugh's big oak tree, standing tall and dark in the snow, at the edge of the hill. "When I think of American liberties, I think of American oak trees," he said. "The kind that grow in our soil grow nowhere else in the world."

He shook hands with Jeremy and Hugh. "I will see your grandfather tomorrow morning," he told them. "Tonight I will find lodging somewhere near, that I may offer Joseph Bonaparte what comfort I can. We must all help him with plans for building his house again, for he must have shelter and a home." He turned about and went in, while the two boys walked across the hard-trodden snow to the drive.

Hugh, remembering something, put his hand into his

pocket and pulled out the scrap of paper which he, for his part, had snatched from the fire. They could just make it out in the fading light, for it was a proclamation of some kind, written very large and clear—

"No person bearing the name of Bonaparte is to enter France again—penalty of death—" Hugh pushed it back into his pocket. There was no need of returning that to Mr. Bonaparte. Hugh would give it, later, to Mr. Girard.

"Look," he cried suddenly to Jeremy, as he glanced up. "See, there on the ridge, where Grandfather's house is."

The sky was growing dusky, but to the east was clearly visible the rise of ground and the outline of Grandfather's long white house from whose terrace they had flown the kite. It was so dark that they could see little but the looming shape, but, as they watched, a spark of brightness appeared, and then another, the whole long row of windows on the terrace was alight, showing one by one.

"It's Grandfather and Mother and Hilda who are up yonder," Hugh said. "They have taken all the candles they could find, and have gone up to the house where we will live again now, to light it up, every window, in honor of your coming home." He could see in his mind's eye how they were going together from room to room, Grandfather moving slowly and carefully but smiling; Mother bright-eyed, erect, and happy; Hilda dashing from window to window with the candles. He had no doubt whose idea it was—most certainly it was Hilda's.

He and Jeremy could see, almost as clearly within their minds, all that was before them now, how they would return to live in the long white house above the river, how Grandfather's business would go forward again, with Grandfather to direct it, with Mr. Girard to advise, but with Jeremy, certainly with Jeremy, to be the real force and spirit of their undertakings. And in time, Hugh, Hugh Armond, would take his own part and share in them. Perhaps they would never find great riches, but they would have part in the world's buying and selling; there would always be work and friends, good friends like Mr. Girard, and John and Betsy Storrs, and Hilda, with her serious eyes, her energetic spirit, and her determination that Hugh should never lag in carrying out the best of everything that was in him.

It looked very good, all that was before them, as they walked together through the great iron gates and out into the road.